All Knight Long, Book I: One Warlock's Love Story
Torquere Press Publishers
1380 Rio Rancho Blvd #1319
Rio Rancho, NM 87124
Copyright 2013 by Shad O. Walker
Cover illustration by BSClay
Published with permission
ISBN: 978-1-61040-585-0

www.torquerepress.com

First Torquere Press Printing: August 2013
Printed in the USA

Shad O. Walker

All Knight Long, Book I: One Warlock's Love Story

All Knight Long, Book I: One Warlock's Love Story by Shad O. Walker

Torquere Press Inc.
romance for the rest of us
www.torquerepress.com

This book is dedicated to the readers who have been with me since the very beginning, the OWLS! Blessed be.

All Knight Long, Book I: One Warlock's Love Story

Chapter 1

Zander Knight was used to keeping secrets. He was, after all, a warlock who lived in a mortal community and had attended a mortal high school. As a general rule, witches and warlocks didn't mix with mortals and most certainly never revealed themselves as such. Zander's former high school friends only knew him as the little guy with the good grades and the great smile, but the elite magical community in the Southeast United States knew that he was special.

His notoriety was due, in part, to the fact that his birth had ended the longstanding feud between the Zander and Knight magical families. His mother, Crystal Zander, was an exotic, doe-eyed, wavy-haired potions worker who could have just as easily passed for Native American as Brazilian. His father, Malachi Knight, was a caramel-colored spellcaster with full, round features and an athletic physique. Crystal and Malachi's first meeting nearly twenty years ago had sparked a love stronger than any magic either of them could have conjured.

The feud between the Zander and Knight families had been legendary and was believed to have been started over a debate about which of the families could trace its magical roots back the furthest. Crystal and Malachi met as teenagers at the annual celebration of love and light called the Litha, where young witches and warlocks gathered at a discreet location at high noon in bright and colorful clothing, and then partied for two consecutive days. They hadn't recognized each other as would-be enemies because their families had always kept them apart, but there was no denying the attraction. By the time they realized that they were from feuding families, they were in love and Crystal was pregnant with Zander. Despite their parents' protests, their love endured and ultimately succeeded in bringing the fighting families into an uneasy alliance.

All the signs spoke of mysterious and wonderful things. Zander was born at midnight on the summer solstice, and every member of both great families was present to give gifts and offer blessings. By the age of seven, Zander had shown a proclivity for potions work and spell casting, and by the age of twelve, he was capable of performing tricks done by warlocks twice his age. His extended family suggested that he attend one of the better private magic schools and eventually vie for one of the Southeastern coven leader positions, yet his parents wanted no part of magical politics and opted to put Zander in a regular mortal high school. Unfortunately, going to a mortal high school didn't afford him an opportunity to hone his magical gifts.

Yes, Zander Knight was used to keeping secrets. He was a sixth generation warlock, who attended a mortal high school... and he was gay.

Chapter 2

Z ander!" Crystal yelled from downstairs of their
large three-story home in rural Georgia. Zander
looked at his alarm clock, shifted in his bed, and
pulled the covers up over his head.

"Zander Borealis Knight!" she yelled again.

"What?" he moaned, knowing full well that she
couldn't hear him from under the covers.

"Your Grandmother Zoe is here, and she wants to
see you," his mother sang. Everyone knew that Zander
adored his maternal grandmother, Zoe Zander. Despite
the fact that he was eighteen years old, he jumped from
the bed like a kid at Christmas and ran down the stairs to
greet his grandmother.

"Look at you! You're still wearing those same old
flannel pajama bottoms, and you're getting so big
and tall!" She embraced him with a hug that only a
grandmother could give.

"Grandma, I'm 5'8" and 147 pounds. I am *not* big
and tall," he laughed.

"Well, you are tall to me," she answered, peering up
at him.

"Look at all of your muscles!" she continued, rubbing
his stomach, spinning him around and then slapping his
backside. Zander smiled. Even he had to admit that he'd

filled out nicely since seeing his grandmother last winter. Going to a mortal high school, instead of a private magic school, hadn't been completely bad. He'd managed to become student body vice president and make the varsity track, tennis, and gymnastics teams. His regular workouts had given him a v-shaped torso, very defined abs, and an ass that looked like two ripe melons.

"Grandma, what are you doing here?" Zander asked.

"I am here for my favorite grandson's eighteenth birthday!" she whispered.

"You didn't have to come all the way from Maryland to Georgia a whole day early. My party isn't until tomorrow."

"I know the party is tomorrow. I also know that all of your daddy's people will be here pulling at you by tomorrow morning, especially your mean old Grandmother Nasha. I need my own special time with you. Now go get dressed and come for a walk in the garden with your favorite grandma," she teased. Zander kissed her on the forehead and ran back upstairs to get showered and dressed.

"Clean up your room and make up your bed before you come back downstairs," his mother yelled.

Zander showered, dressed and stood looking at himself in the mirror the way he used to every morning before heading off to high school. He was wearing jeans, a red t-shirt, and red Tom's. He had worn his naturally wavy hair low and lined for the last year, despite the fact that his mother liked it long and loose. He had his father's caramel complexion, full lips, and strong nose and his mother's dark, piercing eyes. Like all young male warlocks coming into heat around their eighteenth year, his natural body odor was a unique, yet subtle, earthy scent. Zander's smell was a mild patchouli and sage blend that most of his friends at school mistook for body oils.

He didn't dare explain to them that it was the young

warlock's way of attracting a mate. Young girls would secretly find themselves moist with hardened, aching nipples and young guys would have to hide their erections whenever they were around him for long periods of time. It was just another thing about being an 18-year-old warlock that Zander couldn't share with his friends at school. His parents had insisted upon living out in the country and not near one of the nine major private magic schools across the United States. They wanted his life to be as "normal" as possible. The truth was that Zander was far from normal. Despite his limited at-home magical training in the evenings and on the weekends, Zander was an extremely powerful warlock with a unique destiny.

Zander's grandmother was out in the garden talking to the day fairies.

"Grandma!" Zander said, waving his hands and calling up a spell to surround her in a swirling, heart-shaped wreath of flower petals from his mother's garden. She smiled, lifted her hands, and allowed the petals to envelope her.

"I see you are ripening," she said, acknowledging his scent.

"Don't remind me," Zander said, as he forced the petals to take the form of a small bird and fly back off behind the cornstalks. He plopped down into the large swing beside his grandmother.

"You should be elated. You finally graduated from that awful mortal high school, your eighteenth birthday party is tomorrow, and I hear that your parents are going to let you go to the Litha by yourself this year and get your own private tent," she said.

Zander sighed and looked across the multiple rows of herbs that his mother had grown for her potions. "The high school isn't that bad. Mortals aren't that bad."

"You should be around other witches and warlocks

your own age. I've tried to explain that your mother. Do you even have any magical friends?"

"I have one," Zander defended, thinking of Giovanni, a chat room buddy from Atlanta whom he'd met on an Internet dating site for down-low magicals called warlock4warlock.com. They had never met in person, but Giovanni claimed to be an eighteen-year-old warlock who had attended the private magic school in Atlanta until he was kicked out of his house for being gay.

"Does he come from a good family?" Zoe asked.

"Yes," he answered, offering a half-truth.

"Good. You have to be careful these days," she warned. "There are bad witches and warlocks, shape shifters, witch hunters, and vampires out there." Zander was a bit shocked by his grandmother's frankness. He had lived a relatively sheltered life, and his family rarely talked about the dark side of the supernatural community, let alone exposed him to other supernaturals.

"You don't have to become a coven leader. You can go off to Europe and study like some of the other young warlocks of your breeding," she encouraged. Zander didn't reply.

"What is wrong, Butterbean?" she asked. Zander chuckled at the nickname. He hadn't heard it in over ten years.

"Grandma, I am a full-grown warlock, and I've never ever had a real relationship. I've never even kissed anyone," he said, surprising himself with his honesty.

"There are plenty of young witches that would love to date you. I know your parents have got you stuck down here in the country, but young witches at some of the finest private magic schools across the country know about you. Word travels," she explained.

"Okay, Grandma," Zander said.

"What about that fine young witch that your Uncle

Siran had come down from New York to go with you to your prom? She comes from a very fine family of wand workers. I saw the pictures. You two made a very handsome couple."

"Her name was Celestial, and I don't think she was really excited about going to a mortal prom. I'm still wondering how much my parents had to pay her to come all the way down here from New York. I'm not really good in social situations with witches and warlocks outside the family, and I don't even know if I want to go to the Litha," Zander added.

"Then forget the prom and the Litha for now. Think about your birthday party. You know the celebrations are always great family events. I've even learned to tolerate that old nasty Nasha," Zoe said.

"Grandma Nasha isn't that bad," Zander defended.

"Maybe not, but it is a good thing you got your looks and magical gifts from your mother's side of the family," Grandma Zoe said.

"You better be nice. It won't take much for you and Nana Nasha to be fighting out here tomorrow," Zander joked.

"I'm counting on it," she said, and they both laughed.

"So, tell me what has got you so worked up. What are you not telling me?" she asked. Zander didn't reply.

Zoe didn't say a word. Instead, she eased herself up from the swing and slowly walked over to the garden where she began gathering different flowers and herbs. After several minutes of comfortable silence between the two of them, she came back with a floral mixture in her hands and then began clapping and chanting around Zander until a thin, orange haze surrounded him. She swung her arms, and the thin orange cloud began to morph and change colors. She looked into the haze around Zander like a doctor making a diagnosis.

"What are you doing?" he asked, though he knew the answer.

"Reading your aura and seeing your truth," she explained nonchalantly. It was old magic and not easily administered by the unpracticed.

"And?" he asked, hesitantly.

"You tell me," she said, before coming to a halt and giving him a long look.

"I don't think I have to," he said.

"I know that you are hiding something that you've been struggling with for a very long time," she said. "Maybe it is that you don't really like Celestial or any of the young ladies that your parents have selected for you, or maybe you aren't ready to embrace your magical destiny. All I know is that you need to start living your life on your own terms. I made the mistake of living my life for the coven and the call." Zander realized that she was being kind by not telling him everything that she saw. He also figured that she wanted to let him tell her, but he just wasn't ready.

"Grandma, can we keep this little conversation between us?" he pleaded.

"Our secret?" she asked.

"Our secret," he responded. "Is there any chance that anyone else here knows that little spell that you just cast?"

"I am an old witch, but not a dumb witch. I taught most of the witches and warlocks in this family everything that they know, but not everything that *I* know," she said.

They both laughed.

Chapter 3

Zander's birthday party was everything that his grandmother had promised. Three large tents were set up in the expansive yard behind his house. Back in the old days when Zander's family was celebrating his first few birthdays, they'd had one tent for the Zander family, one tent for the Knight family, and a third tent for those who were brave enough to venture into the common tent with Zander and his parents. Over the years, more and more of the family members found their way into the middle tent, leaving one tent for food and the other for Zander's numerous gifts. This, however, was the best birthday party that Zander had ever had. The gift tent was filled with everything from ancient artifacts and magical tomes to designer clothes and electronics. The food tent overflowed with all sorts of natural and organic recipes prepared by the very best cooks in the family, and the music and laughter could be heard from miles around.

By late afternoon, most of the family elders had gathered in the center tent to show off old magic, with Zoe and Nasha right at the center. After all of the gifts had been opened, most of the food had been eaten, the warlock's birthday song had been sung, and Zander's father had offered him blessings, it was time for everyone to go home.

"What do you think, Butterbean?" his Grandmother Zoe asked.

"It was great, Grandma," Zander answered.

"And I didn't have to kill old Nasha," she added.

"Thanks for that," he laughed.

"I heard your father cover you in blessings for your trip to the Litha. Are you ready for your first solo trip?"

"My mother packed my luggage and dad filled my car with gas, so I guess I'm ready to go," he answered.

"That innocent shit might work on your old, cross-eyed Grandma Nasha, but I am the smart grandmother. I don't think for one second that you are going to Atlanta just to go to the Litha," she said, pinching his behind.

"Ouch, Grandma! Damn! That hurt... All right, already. I might have a little *excursion* planned." He glanced around suspiciously, lowering his voice with each word.

"What are you going to tell your parents?" she asked.

"I'm not going to tell them anything other than I am going to the Litha to socialize with all of the young ladies that they have arranged for me to meet. What are you going to tell them?" he asked.

"I'm not going to tell them anything as long you promise to be safe," she answered.

"Our secret?" he asked.

"Our secret."

"Thanks," Zander sighed in relief.

"There is one last thing," Zoe said.

"What's that?"

"I didn't give you your birthday present yet." She smiled.

"You don't have to give me anything," Zander said, sincerely. "You've done enough."

Zoe reached into her pocket and pulled out a brilliant, red ruby stone attached to a leather string and tied it around his neck. Zander admired the piece and gave his grandmother a hug and a kiss. "Thank you," he said, not knowing exactly what it was.

"And don't take it off until I see you again," she ordered.

Chapter 4

The annual Litha was being held in Atlanta, which made it easy for Zander to finally meet his Internet chat buddy Giovanni. The Litha was held at a large, secluded concert campground that was occasionally used for renaissance festivals, alternative concerts, and obscure sporting events. The fact that it was just outside the Atlanta city limits was enough to keep most mortals away, but numerous wards and charms had been placed around the perimeter to discourage mortals from accidentally stumbling upon the event. This year's Litha was particularly festive. The organizers had gone to great lengths to have the best organic delicacies, most popular magical musicians, and most beautifully designed decorations. The weather was perfect, and the early rumors were that they had already reached record attendance levels by the afternoon of the first day.

Zander made it to the celebration site as planned, where he met several of his older cousins, who politely introduced him to a of host eligible young witches that his parents had arranged for him to meet. Despite the fact that they all seemed extremely aroused by his ripening, there wasn't a single one that he found even remotely interesting. He tried his very best to be gracious, sure that each one would send a report back to his family. The crowd was thick enough by nightfall for him to sneak away and give his grandmother a call. As always, she answered before the first ring.

"You'll have to teach me how to do that one day," he said.

"I'll teach you everything that you know, but I won't teach you everything that *I* know," she teased.

"Yes, I remember."

"So, did you meet anyone?" she asked.

"I've met dozens of people, but..." he started.

"...none of them tickled your fancy," she finished.

"You could say that." He sighed.

"So, does the *excursion* begin now?" she whispered.

"I think so."

"Your parents have already started to get reports back from the families in Atlanta. You've been doing a very good job of faking it. The crowd should be large enough now for you to sneak way, but what are you going to do when your cousins Waverly, Vera, and the rest of them come looking for you?" she asked.

"I have my own private tent here at the campsite. I'll tell them that I was still tired from my birthday party and I went to lay down," he said.

"You did get your smarts from my side of the family," she proclaimed.

"Yes, I did."

"Do you have on the protective charm that I gave you?" she asked.

"What?" he asked.

"The necklace," she reminded him. He reached down into his shirt and grabbed the ruby, and for the first time he noticed that it seemed cool to the touch.

"Of course I do," he told her.

"Good. Don't take it off!" she ordered again.

"I won't. I promise. Are you sure you haven't told anyone about this?"

"I am a ride or die witch. I've got you," she teased, doing a pretty good impression of sounding like someone a fraction of her age.

"I am going to meet my friend Giovanni, and then I'm—"

"Stop. The less you tell me, the better. I've been reading the tea leaves and throwing bones for the last two days. Tonight will be a turning point for you, and it is going to be filled with magic and excitement. Embrace it."

"Thanks, Grandma." Zander sighed and ended the call.

Chapter 5

It was just before midnight when Zander arrived in Giovanni's neighborhood. Giovanni lived in a pricey condo right in the center of Atlantic Station, a mixed-use neighborhood on the northwestern edge of Midtown Atlanta. From his profile, Giovanni was about Zander's height and complexion but with much sharper features, a goatee, and shoulder-length dreadlocks. Giovanni had promised to meet Zander in front of the H&M clothing store in Atlantic Station. When Zander drove up, Giovanni was standing there looking just like he did in the pictures from his online profile.

Zander's nerves took over as soon as he saw Giovanni. He had never actually hung out with another warlock who wasn't a cousin or family member. And his relatives always seemed to only tolerate him and talk down to him. Zander and Giovanni's online chatting had started out like most online conversations, filled with flirtatious banter and innuendo, but had quickly turned into something more like a friendship after they started to share personal problems. Giovanni was learning to live on his own after having been outed to his family by a magic school classmate, and Zander was struggling with being a closeted gay warlock living among mortal teenagers.

Despite the friendship, Zander couldn't help but notice

how attractive and confident Giovanni seemed, standing on the corner in skinny jeans and purple combat boots. A necklace of purple beads hung around his neck, both of his wrists were filled with multi-colored bracelets halfway up his arms, and all but four of his fingers were covered in rings. Both of his ears were pierced, and the phrase "MAGIC TRICK," was tattooed on the lower left side of his neck.

Zander stopped at the curb in front of Giovanni at the H&M store.

"Love and light!" Giovanni said, jumping into the passenger's seat as if they had known each other for years. Zander extended his hand for a shake, and Giovanni responded by reaching across the seat and giving him a big hug.

"Blessed be," Zander responded.

"Nice to finally meet you face to face, Z. You *are* a cutie!" Giovanni exclaimed, punching him in the arm.

"Thank you. You aren't so bad yourself." Zander smiled.

"I like your car," Giovanni offered, looking around Zander's Audi. The new black A6 had been a graduation gift from his parents.

"I like your neighborhood," Zander volleyed.

"Thanks. I live right there in that building." Giovanni pointed to the largest building in the center of the courtyard.

"How can you afford to live in a place like that on your own?" Zander wondered.

"I am a sexy, young warlock. The world is mine! You know most witches and warlocks don't work. Why should I be any different?" Giovanni opened his arms, allowing his bracelets and bangles to jingle.

"I know, but most of us have family money that has been built up over the years. I thought you said your family kicked you out with nothing."

"I'll admit that I've had to be resourceful," Giovanni explained.

"Do you miss your family?" Zander asked carefully.

"Fuck them," Giovanni responded, without missing a beat.

"Okay, so where are we going?" Zander asked, changing the conversation before the mood could get too heavy.

"We are going to teach you how to be a young warlock in the city. I can tell that you are ripe, too. I love it," Giovanni teased, taking a moment to sniff him. Zander blushed and wondered if this was how all young warlocks in heat acted. Their collective scents filled the car with the force of a dozen new air fresheners. Zander's patchouli and sage mixed with Giovanni's sandalwood and lavender to create a mindboggling symphony of smells. Zander had never been in such close proximity with another ripening warlock, and the effect was damn near overwhelming. His cock stiffened in his pants, his nipples poked through his shirt, and he was starting to perspire.

Zander rolled down the window and asked again, "So, where does one go to learn how to become a young warlock in the city?"

Giovanni took another deep breath before responding. "There's a brand new club just south of the city for folks like us."

"For warlocks?"

"For warlocks, witches, shifters, vamps and any other supernaturals!"

"Is that safe?" Zander asked. "I thought we didn't mix."

"The old folk don't mix. It's a new day. Our generation doesn't care as much. It's kind of like racism. Besides, there's no magic, shifting, or biting allowed in the club," Giovanni explained.

"Biting?" Zander asked. Giovanni laughed, directed Zander toward the highway, and turned the radio volume up to hear D'Angelo's latest single.

"What do you have to worry about?" Giovanni asked. "You're wearing a magic ruby stone around your neck. Someone very powerful must really love you. They don't come easy."

"Yeah, thanks," Zander said, not realizing that the gift that his grandmother had given him was quite so special.

The ripening scent reached a fevered pitch. Without a word, Giovanni pulled a packet of wet naps from his pocket, reclined the passenger's seat, and pulled out his eight-inch, uncut dick and started masturbating.

"What are you doing?" Zander asked, alarmed.

"What do you mean? Your scent is driving me crazy. My ripening keeps me horny, but you are something else. Don't you ever masturbate?" Giovanni asked, stroking even harder.

"Yes, but not in my car," Zander said desperately.

"Just drive. I'll go crazy if I don't do something about this right now. We can pull over beside the road and jack off together if you want," Giovanni offered.

"That's okay," Zander said, glancing back and forth between the highway and Giovanni's beautiful hooded dick. Giovanni leaned over several times to smell Zander. It didn't take long for him to climax and shoot a huge load onto Zander's dashboard and windshield.

"What are you doing? My dad is going to kill me," Zander screamed.

"It's come, not acid. It'll wipe right off." Giovanni cleaned himself before wiping down Zander's automobile interior.

"Do you want me to drive while you get yours? The

last thing you want to do is walk up in a club with all those cute boys as ripe as you are. There's no telling what might happen," Giovanni warned.

"I'll be fine." Zander started to wonder if finally meeting Giovanni was such a good idea.

"Suit yourself," Giovanni said, reaching into his pocket and pulling out a joint. He cast a quick fire spell, lit the joint, inhaled, and laid back.

"Are you serious?" Zander asked incredulously.

"My fault. Do you want some?" Giovanni handed the fat joint to Zander.

"You can't smoke in here. My parents don't allow smoking in here!" Zander squealed. His voice was higher than he intended.

"You are very uptight," Giovanni announced. "I think you need some dick!"

"Just put out the marijuana," Zander warned. Giovanni took one last drag, before putting out the joint and slipping it back into his pocket. He slumped down in the seat, folded his arms, and poked out his bottom lip. The next few miles were filled with awkward silence until Zander broke the ice.

"I'm sorry," he said.

"I forgive you," Giovanni perked up immediately, leaned over, and gave Zander a huge kiss on the cheek. They both laughed out loud.

"We're almost there. Take the next exit, go through the next five lights and take a right. It'll be the large abandoned-looking warehouse at the end of the street," Giovanni instructed.

"Got it," Zander said, glad that they were speaking again.

"So, I never asked. What power level are you?" Giovanni questioned

"I never took the formal private magic school leveling

exam, but I test out at a 10.6 on the home exam," Zander said.

"Damn! Are you serious? 10.6 out of 12? That is coven leader level. I don't even think I know anyone in double digits. 10.6 and you aren't even out of your teens!"

"It isn't really that big a deal," Zander mumbled.

"Damn if it isn't. At a 10.6 you're able to handle levitation and transformation, right?" Giovanni asked.

"I am actually thinking about going to Europe for formal training," Zander said, surprising himself. He hadn't really been thinking about going to Europe, but it sounded good, so he went with it. He also wasn't that good at magic. Sure he was powerful, but he had never been trained to wield magic the way that his cousins had at the private magic schools.

"That's wassup! Hell, I might even go with you. I'm not trying to do any damn studying, but I am sure that there are a few hot boys in Europe ready for a little *magic trick*," he teased.

"I think we're here," Zander said, looking at the cars parked along both sides of the street leading up to the large warehouse at the end of the road.

"This is it. Now we just need to find somewhere to park. Turn up this side street. I think I see a space on the other side of that truck." Sure enough, there was a space just large enough for Zander's A6, and he parallel parked with relative ease.

"I think we need to leave our valuables in the car. These types of clubs can attract some shady characters," Giovanni said.

"What?" Zander asked, immediately wary.

"It isn't a tea party or a tired-ass Litha." Giovanni rolled his eyes. "This is a real fucking club. All you need is some money and your ID."

"What kind of place is this again?" Zander asked, his

nerves welling up in his stomach.

"It's an underground club for same-sex loving supernaturals called Arcane," Giovanni said lightly, as he jumped out of the car and slammed the door. Zander stuffed all of his valuables, except $40 and his identification, in the glove compartment and then locked and covered it with a small protection spell. Giovanni was halfway up the street before Zander could even get out of the car.

"Wait! Did you say same-sex loving?" Zander asked, looking around cautiously. The night was completely still and unusually bright. Zander found himself wishing that he had paid more attention to his grandmother's lessons on communicating with night fairies. One person was making his way toward the club from the other end of the street, and he didn't seem to be very interested in either Zander or Giovanni. The large warehouse stood still and silent, and Zander was starting to wonder if they were at the right place.

"Maybe we should just..." Zander began.

"Just what? Loosen up your look a little bit?" Giovanni unbuttoned and removed Zander's striped dress shirt, leaving him in a cerulean t-shirt, jeans, and running shoes. Giovanni picked through the dozens of bracelets lining his arms and decided on six to slide onto Zander's right wrist. Giovanni threw Zander's discarded dress shirt in the air, waved his hand, and watched it disappear in a puff of smoke.

"Why did you do that?" Zander asked, annoyed.

"We're going to a club, not an interview," Giovanni replied simply. "Do you not have any tattoos or piercings?"

"No," Zander said defensively.

"Don't you ever wear any jewelry?" he continued.

"Not really," Zander answered.

"We can work on that later. Now you look like

someone that I might hang out with. Let's go!" Giovanni grabbed Zander's hand and jogged up the street.

Zander hadn't noticed before, but a massive, bulky bodyguard, clad in all black with a blonde Mohawk and sunglasses was now standing at the front entrance to Arcane.

"Where did he come from?" Zander whispered.

"Be quiet," Giovanni whispered. "She'll hear you. That's a shape shifter." Zander took Giovanni's lead as they approached the burly bodyguard, who wore a nametag that indicated her name was Ooba.

Giovanni lifted his arms to be frisked. The bodyguard took a long whiff and an even longer time giving him a body search. Giovanni, however, seemed to enjoy it. Zander endured a similar sniff and search routine before they were allowed to enter. The bodyguard's deep, sultry baritone boomed, "Glad that you two came out tonight. Nothing tastes quite as good as ripe warlock." Zander felt the cool ruby on his chest heat up like it had been set on fire.

As soon as they crossed the threshold from the outside to the inside of the club, they went from complete silence to raucous club noise the likes of which Zander had never heard. There was screaming, laughing, and howling covered by a thick layer of typical club music. The music's heavy liquid vocal harmonies and intricate melodic phrasing seemed to seep into Zander's soul. They entered into a long, narrow hallway filled with dozens of people waiting to get into the club. The walls were covered with handwritten signs reading NO SHIFTING, NO SPELL CASTING, NO SUCKING! The air was filled with an intoxicating mixture of marijuana, alcohol, and some other musky sent that Zander couldn't quite identify.

Despite the narrow hallway, several people at the end of the line turned to look at Zander and Giovanni as soon as they came in. The bodyguard slammed the door behind them, forcing Zander to bump into Giovanni, who was already beginning to gyrate and dance to the music.

"What is everyone looking at?" Zander whispered to Giovanni.

"I think they smelled us before they saw us. You *are* pretty ripe, and I am fine as hell. When was the last time you busted a nut anyway? The longer you go without sex, the riper you will become. You know that." Giovanni exchanged flirtatious glances with a tall, slim, Asian vampire further up in the line.

"I know," Zander said, but he really didn't.

"It has been a while since I have had sex with a vampire. They fuck like rabbits in heat. I am getting hard again just thinking about it. He is gorgeous, and his body is as hot as fire. Do you think he has a nice dick?" Giovanni asked, never taking his eyes off of the vamp.

"What? No!" Zander hissed.

The line moved fairly quickly. When they reached the front, a beautiful, coffee-colored, young vampiress behind a glass enclosure recited the same rules that were plastered on the walls. The only difference was that she also gave the warning that they would be neutralized and permanently banned from the club if they were caught violating any of them. Zander didn't know what it meant to be neutralized, but he knew that he didn't want it done to him. After they agreed to follow the rules, the vampiress asked each of them to present identification and $20. After Zander showed his driver's license and Giovanni showed his magic school identification, they were escorted through a large, black curtain by a figure in a dark, hooded robe.

The club was huge, and every inch seemed packed with writhing and wiggling bodies. Zander's heart rate increased as the ruby went white hot against his skin.

It was so hot, in fact, that he took it off and stuffed it into his pocket. Men were dancing with men, women were dancing with women, vampires were dancing with shifters, and shifters were dancing with witches. Zander noticed that the dances that they were doing were nothing like the ones that he and his mortal friends did back at his old high school dances. Someone howled behind them, and Zander jumped.

"Let's go get a drink! Maybe that will loosen you up," Giovanni laughed. Zander could barely hear him over the club music. Giovanni grabbed Zander's hand and pulled him through the thrashing crowd toward the bar. Hands grabbed at every part of Zander's body as they made their way through. He kept checking to make sure that his necklace, ID, and cash were still in his pocket.

The bar was at the other end of the club, furthest away from the DJ and dance floor, so it was just a little bit easier for Zander to hear.

"This shit is crazy!" Giovanni yelled.

"That is an understatement," Zander sighed. The bar, like the rest of the club, was crowded, but Giovanni wasn't shy about shoving his way up toward the front. A young, warlock bartender with shoulder length, blond hair immediately noticed them.

"Love and light," he said, acknowledging Zander and Giovanni with the traditional warlocks' greeting. They both responded with, "Blessed be."

"My name is Milo. What are two little ripe warlocks like yourselves doing in a place like this?"

"Milo, my name is Giovanni, and this is Zander. We are here celebrating my friend's eighteenth birthday," Giovanni said. Zander smiled.

"No wonder you are so ripe. You just turned eighteen. You two had better not stand in one place for too long. You might get felt up in here," Milo teased.

"Where does the line start?" Giovanni asked, and Milo laughed. Just then, the tall, slim, Asian vampire from the line slid up behind Giovanni.

"Bartender, these drinks are on me," he said, pointing to Giovanni and Zander.

"We don't know you," Giovanni said, coyly.

"You don't know me *yet*," the vampire corrected. He looked to be around twenty-five in human years. He had a model's swagger, a swimmer's build, and he oozed of sensuality.

"I'm Giovanni and this is my friend, Zander. It's his birthday," Giovanni announced again. The vampire gave Zander a polite look and moved closer to Giovanni.

"My name is Hung," he said.

"Really?" Giovanni raised an eyebrow.

"Hung is Vietnamese for spirit of a hero," he explained.

"Oh, I thought it was vampire for you have a big dick," Giovanni said.

"That, too." Hung smiled, staring at the pulsing jugular in Giovanni's neck.

"What are you having?" Milo interrupted, from behind the bar.

"I'll have a Bloody Mary—type O," Hung said.

"Give us Hennessy and hemlock," Giovanni said. Hung paid, and Milo poured the drinks and slammed them on the counter. Giovanni gulped down his drink before Zander could properly thank Hung. Hung whispered something in Giovanni's ear, and Giovanni turned to Zander.

"I'm going to go dance with Hung. Stay here. I'll be right back," Giovanni assured him. He was gone before Zander could object. Zander turned toward Milo, who was giving him a sympathetic smile.

"I'll watch you until your friend gets back. Your next drink is on me since it's your birthday," Milo winked.

Zander couldn't tell if it was pity or flirting, but it didn't matter. He would take either at this point. Zander reached into his pocket to find that the stone was even hotter. So hot, in fact, that it was starting to burn his leg. He reached up to the bar, grabbed a few napkins, wrapped the ruby necklace several times, and stuffed it back in his pocket.

Zander could see Giovanni grinding his fat little ass on Hung's dick in the center of the dance floor. It was a good thing that no one had asked him to dance because he wasn't sure that he could move that seductively without some practice and a few more drinks. He took a sip of his cocktail and was pleasantly surprised at how the smooth potion warmed him up and lowered his inhibitions. He'd tasted alcohol before but had never had his own drink – and certainly not one with hemlock in it. He stood with his back to the bar, occasionally smiling at admirers and trying to make sense of Club Arcane.

The DJ booth was perched up on a crow's nest on the opposite end of the club behind a dark, smoky glass. Zander couldn't see the DJ, but he could tell from the music that whoever was in there knew how to stir a crowd. The dance floor was shaped like a large square with pairs of male and female strippers dancing in cages in each of the four corners. Several platforms at different heights peppered the floor for dancers who wanted to see and be seen. To the left was the black curtain through which they had entered, and to the right was a series of numbered doors that were being patrolled by other security guards dressed like Ooba. The music changed into something with more of a reggae feel. Zander looked back toward the dance floor to find Giovanni and Hung now up on one of the platforms swinging and swaying to the beat.

Zander swallowed his entire drink and allowed the warm feeling to ease through his body.

"Not too fast, young warlock," Milo said, as he slid another glass of Hennessy and hemlock toward Zander.

"Okay," Zander agreed. He grabbed the second drink and took a small sip before turning his attention back toward Giovanni, Hung, and the undulating crowd. He could feel the Hennessy and hemlock opening him up. Zander wasn't a bad dancer. He just wasn't familiar with these particular dances. He studied Giovanni and imagined himself doing those same moves. Zander took the second drink and gulped it down.

"If you take it slow, then it might not hurt so much in the morning," a voice said from behind Zander. He turned to find himself staring into a very broad and well-formed chest. Zander looked up into a pair of light brown eyes and was speechless. The stranger was tall and extremely muscular with skin the color of milk chocolate. He wore his hair in a long Afro, which was adorned with one cowrie shell at his left temple. A small, hemp loop was threaded through his right ear like an earring. His tight, white t-shirt seemed to show every single muscle in his torso, and his fitted jeans were doing nothing less for his legs and ass. The bulge at his crotch looked like he had stuffed a pair of socks or a large sausage in his pants. Zander assumed from his designer leather boots that he might also own a motorcycle.

"Excuse me?" Zander asked, trying not to stare into his eyes.

"I said if you take it slow, then it might not hurt so much in the morning," the stranger repeated. Zander hesitated a second before realizing that he was referring to how quickly he had downed his second drink. Milo was no longer behind the bar, and Giovanni and Hung were nowhere to be found. Zander was all out of liquid courage and standing face to face with the most handsome man that he had ever seen.

"You look frightened. Is there something wrong?" His voice poured over Zander like warm honey. He felt his dick hardening in his jeans and wondered if his ripening scent was becoming more noticeable.

"There's nothing wrong. I was just looking for my friend," Zander said, leaning back against the bar. The stranger moved in a little closer and placed his right hand on the bar just behind Zander's back.

"He must be a pretty careless friend to lose a nice piece like you," he said.

"He's not that kind of friend, and I am not a *piece*," Zander said haughtily.

"My apologies. I just smelled... I mean saw you when you came in, and I had to take advantage of this opportunity to come over and introduce myself."

"That was very nice of you," Zander said, staring at his full lips and exceptionally white teeth.

"My name is Zuri Tau Long. My friends call me Tau," he said.

"Nice to meet you, Tau. My name is Zander," he responded, realizing that this is what he had been imagining since he had started to ripen—a chance to flirt like all of the other kids back at his high school. Although he had had two rather strong drinks, he remembered his parents' warning that a witch or a warlock never gave a stranger, especially a magical, his or her full name upon introduction.

Zander knew that name offering given too freely could be used for spell casting. Given the fact that Tau had told Zander his full name, Zander assumed that he must not be a warlock. Zander took a sip and looked up again, noticing Tau's rather long canine teeth. How had Giovanni been able to read other supernaturals so easily? He really should have paid more attention to the training his parents gave him in the evenings and on weekend.

Maybe his grandmother was right. Maybe he should have gone to a private magic school.

"It is very nice to meet you, Zander," Tau said with a chuckle.

"What's so funny?" Zander asked.

"You warlocks and your name offering," Tau said.

"Do you have something against warlocks?" Zander asked.

"Not when they're as ripe as you are and have asses like yours, I don't." Tau winked.

"Excuse me?" Zander said.

"My apologies. My animal side gets the better of me sometime. You have to admit that you are as ripe as hell. Every man in here, and half of the women, have noticed you," Tau said. Zander blushed.

"So, you must be like a shifter—like a werewolf," Zander surmised.

"No, not a werewolf." Tau sounded slightly put out. Zander hoped that he hadn't caused offense. He certainly didn't want him to walk away, so he tried his best to keep the conversation going.

"It's pretty crowded in here tonight, isn't it?" Zander asked.

Tau laughed again, "Of course it's crowded tonight. You magicals have your little Litha in town this week. Word on the street is that the vamps just hit up several of the local blood banks and made off with a big haul of AB negative blood, which means they're in rare form. And there's a full moon tonight. Every supernatural in here is horny as hell. You fanning your little ripe ass all around the club isn't helping much, either."

Zander didn't know if he should be offended or flattered.

"You don't get out too much, do you?" Tau asked.

"So what if I don't?" Zander said, defensively.

"It's cute. Makes me want to take care of you," Tau admitted.

"So... back to you. You are a shifter right?" Zander asked.

"Yes, but you don't have to worry. I won't hurt you," Tau assured him.

"Who said I was worried about you hurting me? I'm a pretty powerful warlock. Maybe you're the one who should be worried," Zander said, trying to sound tough. Tau started laughing before Zander could finish the sentence. His laugh was hearty and pleasant, and it made Zander laugh, too.

"Okay, little warlock. How about you let me buy you another drink?" Tau asked. Zander only had $20 left, and another drink couldn't hurt, could it?

"Is everything all right over here?" Milo appeared back behind the bar. Zander turned and nodded.

"How about you get us two more drinks," Tau said. "A Hennessy and hemlock for my friend, and a peach Ciroc with catnip for me." Milo moved away without responding to Tau or taking his eyes off Zander. When Milo came back with the drinks, Tau threw a $20 bill on the bar and turned back toward Zander. Zander gave Milo an awkward smile.

"How about a toast to... taking it slow so that it doesn't hurt in the morning," Tau said. Zander laughed and took a sip of his drink. Conversely, Tau threw his peach Ciroc and catnip back in one gulp and slammed the cup back on the counter. Zander wasn't sure, but he thought he caught Tau sniffing him.

The music reached a fevered pitch, and the crowd went wild. Tau grabbed Zander's hand. "Would you like to dance?"

"I don't know. I don't get out much, remember?" Zander was half afraid that any attempt to dance would either send Tau away or make him burst into laughter again. Zander put his drink back down on the counter.

"Don't worry. I'll take good care of you. I promise." Tau pulled Zander toward the center of the dance floor, and Zander couldn't help but follow him. When they reached the center of the floor, Zander took a deep breath and tried to decide if he was going to try to emulate Giovanni or simply do one of the dances that he did back at his high school. Neither option seemed very appealing. Before he could make a decision, Tau pulled him in close and began rocking him to the beat. Being so close to Tau felt... *good*. In fact, it was one of the best feelings Zander had ever experienced. They moved together with a rhythm that Zander didn't think possible. He could smell Tau's warm breath on his face, could see Tau's nipples hardening beneath the shirt; he could hear Tau's heart beating over the music, and he could feel Tau's rock-hard body against his—and it wasn't just Tau's body that was hard. Tau's dick was hard as stone, pressed against his stomach. Tau nuzzled and kissed Zander's ear while his hands slipped down toward the small of Zander's back.

"You smell great," Tau said.

"Thank you," Zander hummed.

"You feel good," Tau continued.

"So do you," Zander said, looking pointedly at Tau's massive erection pressed against his abdomen.

"That's your fault for being so damn sexy," Tau teased.

"It's just because I'm ripe right now. I tend to have that effect on people. I'm sure that if I wasn't peaking, you probably wouldn't even have noticed me," Zander looked away.

"Is that what you think? First of all, I'm a shifter. I could smell you even if you weren't ripening, but I do really like your particular scent. Second, I like talking to you. Third, you have a really fat ass!" Tau laughed, grabbing two handfuls of Zander's ass. Zander surprised himself by reaching up and giving Tau a long kiss. It was his first real kiss, and it was more powerful than any magic that he had ever felt. Zander wasn't sure if he was so uninhibited because of the alcohol, the fact that he had met the sexiest man in the club, or both.

"Whoa! Is that what happens when I grab your booty?" Tau asked.

"No. The next time you might get slapped or worse. You seem to keep forgetting that I am a warlock." Zander nibbled on Tau's earlobe. The alcohol was definitely starting to have an effect; Zander could tell he was being much more affectionate than normal.

"Hey! What's going on here?" Giovanni yelled, poking Zander in the side and forcing him to jump. Zander turned and gave Giovanni a huge hug. He could have sworn that he heard Tau growl. Giovanni was holding his new vampire boy toy by the hand, and he looked tipsy. Zander had no idea that vampires could even get drunk.

"What's wrong with him?" Zander asked Giovanni.

"What do you mean?"

"Is he okay?" Zander nodded toward Hung. Giovanni tilted his head back revealing a series of bite marks all along his neck. One was right over his tattoo.

"I let him bite me. You know that a warlock's blood makes vamps drunk, don't you?"

Zander didn't get a chance to answer. Tau was standing behind him, clearing his throat and looking rather impatient.

"Who's the Thundercat?" Giovanni whispered, glancing over at Tau. Tau's demeanor changed from flirtatious to fearsome, indicating that he might have heard Giovanni even through the loud club music.

"What?" Zander asked. Giovanni extended his hand to Tau. "I'm Zander's buddy. My name is Giovanni, and this is my new special friend Hung." Hung gave a stupefied wave, and Tau seemed to relax when he realized that Giovanni and Hung were together.

"This is my friend, Tau," Zander told Giovanni.

"And exactly how many drinks have *you* had?" Giovanni asked Zander in his ear.

"Just one," Zander lied.

"Witch, please," Giovanni teased.

"Okay, three," he responded, hugging Giovanni again. They both laughed.

"I'm going to get Hung some fresh air. It's one thing for a vampire to drink from a warlock. It's something else entirely for a vampire to drink from a ripening warlock." Giovanni rolled his eyes. "He'll probably be like this for a few hours."

"Is he going to be okay?" Zander asked.

"He'll just be really horny when he comes around, and that's when the real fun begins," he said, giving Zander a wink.

Tau began biting his bottom lip and tapping his foot. Zander grabbed Tau's hands from behind and pulled him close so that Tau's erection rested just atop his round booty. The gesture of affection seemed to calm Tau and make his dick grow even larger.

"Be careful with Hung," Zander warned.

"I've got this. You be careful," Giovanni warned. "You're the one dancing with the wild animal. Shifters are no joke. They go in for real, and they play for keeps," He kissed Zander on the cheek and dragged Hung off toward one of the numbered doors. Zander wondered what was behind it.

Just then, Tau kissed the back of Zander's neck and started grinding his huge dick into Zander's back. Zander turned, playfully pushed Tau away, and began dancing so smoothly that he surprised himself. The drinks, the freedom, and Tau's attention were making him feel alive—and sexy. From Tau's reaction, he must have looked pretty good doing it. Zander quickly realized that Tau was a decent dancer, too. As a matter of fact, he was a great dancer, and he moved with surprising agility. If the stares from nearby dancers were any indication, then they must have looked like quite a pair.

Zander was so caught up in the moment that he failed to realize that he was actually levitating several inches off the ground. When other dancers started to notice, Tau grabbed him and carried him off the dance floor.

"There's no magic allowed in the club," Tau grunted in Zander's ear.

"I'm sorry. I got carried away," Zander whispered back. He couldn't help but notice the judgmental stares as they exited the dance floor. Tau set Zander down once they were in the far corner, near the bathrooms.

"I am really sorry," Zander repeated. Tau was still holding his hands.

"It's okay. I don't think any of the security guards noticed."

"Good." Zander sighed with relief.

"Levitation, huh? Maybe you are a pretty powerful little warlock. You may not need my protection after all," Tau teased.

"Mr. Long," Zander said with a smile, "we've been dancing all night, and I barely know anything about you."

"I didn't know that a background check was a prerequisite for a dance," Tau responded.

"Maybe it isn't, but I would like to know more about you," Zander said, secretly hoping that there would be more to his relationship with Tau than just one dance.

"Then ask away but only after you tell me your full name. I understand that witches don't give out their names freely, but I have to know that you trust me."

Zander took a deep breath. "My name is Zander Borealis Knight."

"It's a pleasure to meet you," Tau responded.

"Uh, okay. Where to start?" Zander wondered. "First, how old are you?"

"I am ninety-two seasons," Tau said.

"I know this... Werewolves count their age in seasons. There are four seasons in every year, so that means that you're... 23?"

"Right about the age. Wrong about me being a damn werewolf—again." Tau corrected.

"I am sorry, so are you from Atlanta?" Zander asked, quickly changing the topic. Could the man of his dreams have only been a few hours away his entire life?

"No, I'm from upstate New York. How about you?" Tau countered.

"A small town in Georgia just a few hours from here. What brings you here tonight?" Zander asked.

"Same thing that brings any of us out. This is one of the only clubs on the east coast for same-sex loving supernaturals. The owners have done a good job of getting the word out through underground channels and invoking the necessary protective charms for the club. I've heard about it for a while, and I just wanted to see it for myself."

"I wonder why there aren't more clubs like this," Zander mused aloud.

"There are probably lots of reasons. The balance between supernaturals is pretty delicate. Warlocks, vampires, and shifters haven't always gotten along. And then there's the whole homosexual thing." Tau took the back of his large hand and gently rubbed Zander's arm. Zander appreciated the gesture and smiled in response.

"What do you mean?" he asked.

"For a warlock of your apparent breeding, you don't

seem to know a whole lot about the supernatural world. What happened? Didn't you pay attention in that little magic school you went to?"

"It's a long story," Zander sighed.

"I want to hear it," Tau said, pulling Zander close enough for him to smell the Ciroc and catnip on his breath.

"My parents were from two magical families that had been feuding for years," Zander began. "When they met and fell in love, it was all they could do to keep their parents and grandparents from killing each other. My parents ended up leaving the magical community altogether. They moved to a small town in Georgia and raised me in the mortal ways. They trained me in magic on the evenings and weekends but just the basics."

"It's really unfortunate that you didn't get a chance to learn everything about your heritage and history growing up," Tau said.

"It wasn't very well received by my extended family," Zander admitted. "How about you? How did you grow up?"

"Like most shifters, I grew up in the country," Tau explained. "My family owns a ranch in upstate New York. I was home-schooled."

"I am glad that we met tonight," Zander said, considering for the first time that Tau might be one of those players that the bitter, broken-hearted divas always wailed about in song.

"I am too," Tau said, sounding sincere.

Just then the vampiress from the door passed by. "You two make a lovely couple," she said. Zander blushed, grinned and thanked her. Seconds later, a waiter brought over two drinks.

"These are from the boss, Muslee," he said, and handed them two cocktails. Tau tried to offer him a tip, but he wouldn't accept it.

"That was nice," Zander said.

"See, I told you everybody in here was looking at you," Tau said. Zander smiled.

"So, you were telling me about the relationships among the three major supernatural groups..." Zander was extremely curious.

"You really don't know this stuff, do you?" Tau said.

"Not really," Zander admitted.

"Aw, baby, come here, and I'll tell you everything you need to know." Tau wrapped Zander is his muscular arms.

"The three major supernatural groups are witches, vampires, and shifters, and at some point in our long and sordid pasts, we have all loved and hated each other. I can explain all of the background and history to you later, but for now you need to focus on the highlights," Tau said, matter-of-factly. Zander was glad to hear that there would be a later.

"We can start with your little ratchet-ass friend, Ginger Snap," Tau continued.

"Giovanni," Zander corrected.

"Yes, her. Anyway, everyone knows that a witch or warlock's blood will intoxicate a vampire and make him very horny, which is pretty dangerous because vampires are known to be very sexual creatures anyway."

"Oh!" Zander said.

"Vamps and shifters have had a long standing feud over who rules the night and how best to harvest humans for food. Over time, the vamps moved into the cities, and the shifters moved out to the rural areas, so there's been less of an issue."

"This is fascinating," Zander said, taking a sip of his drink.

"I'm surprised you don't know this," Tau remarked.

"It was a famous warlock—Banning Cabiness—who popularized the study of supernatural relationships."

"I'm starting to realize that there's a quite a bit that I don't know," Zander admitted.

"Not to worry, little warlock," Tau said. Zander instinctively moved in and put his head on Tau's chest. Tau responded by giving him a huge hug.

"Is it all right if I give you something?"

"What do you mean?" Zander asked, pulling back from Tau's warm embrace.

"I've really enjoyed meeting you, and I don't want you to forget me." Tau removed the cowrie shell from the small lock of hair at his temple and took the hemp earring from his ear.

"What are you doing?" Zander asked. Tau's large hands were more nimble than Zander might have imagined. He took the cowrie shell and the hemp and fashioned a ring that fit perfectly on Zander's right ring finger.

"This shell was given to me by grandfather. They were used as currency in Africa and even thought by some to be magical agents," Tau said.

"That is so sweet," Zander said. "I can't take something that's this valuable to you,"

"I want you to have it," Tau insisted, admiring the ring on Zander's finger.

"I won't feel right unless I give you something of equal value in return. I have a special gift that my grandmother gave me for my birthday. It would mean a lot to me if you would have it. That way I know you won't forget me, either." Zander removed the ruby stone necklace from his pocket and tied it around Tau's neck. It was the second time that Zander had acted against his better judgment in one night. He'd given Tau his full name and his grandmother's birthday gift.

"This is a very special night for me," Tau beamed, giving Zander another kiss.

"So there you are!" Giovanni yelled. Zander was sure that he heard Tau growl this time. Zander turned to greet Giovanni.

"Where's your friend?" Zander asked.

"Apparently, I am too much warlock for him. I sent him to my house to sleep it off. That'll guarantee me some good sex when I get home." Giovanni winked.

"How's he going to find your house, let alone get in without the key?" Zander asked skeptically.

"He's a vampire, silly. He's tasted me. He can find me anywhere on earth now. I gave him my address and invited him to enter my home, so he won't have a problem getting in."

"You should be more responsible," Tau told him. "There are rules in this club for a reason. You shouldn't have let him bite you."

"Who the hell are you supposed to be?" Giovanni asked.

"You recklessness could end up getting Zander into trouble," Tau warned.

"Zander is a warlock. He doesn't need an extra from the Wiz to take care of him," Giovanni said.

"What?" Tau asked, clearly confused.

"You heard me," Giovanni snapped, stepping back to cast a curse. Tau growled and stepped forward.

"Wait! You two can't do that in here. No magic and shifting, remember?" Zander stepped between them and placed his hands on their chests.

"What is that?" Giovanni asked, looking at the new ring on Zander's finger.

"What?" Zander asked, confused at Giovanni's shocked expression.

"Who gave you that ring?" Giovanni asked, gazing skeptically at Tau.

"Tau gave it to me. It's just a keepsake. It's no big deal," Zander said.

"Did you give him anything in return?" Giovanni asked.

"Why do you ask?" Zander questioned, still not sure why it was such a big deal. He also couldn't help but notice that Giovanni's line of questioning seemed to be making Tau slightly uneasy.

"Maybe I underestimated you," Giovanni purred.

Just then, there was a loud explosion on the far end of the club, followed by shrieks, screams, and howls. The building shook, the ceiling caved in, and pandemonium ensued. Giovanni spun around and began moving his arms around in fluid movements. He finished the spell with an incantation that covered both him and Zander with a translucent protective bubble. Hunks of mortar and brick fell from the ceiling, bouncing off Giovanni's shield. Giovanni seemed to get just a little bit weaker each time a piece of rubble struck. Zander looked through the shield and saw a witch levitating trying to avoid the falling debris and several vampires shadow walking out of the room. Shifters were changing quickly, in order to assume the size and speed necessary to withstand whatever was attacking the club. Then he remembered Tau.

Giovanni yelled something, but Zander didn't pay attention. He was too focused on finding Tau. Zander turned to find the once beautiful, muscular Tau transforming into a larger, feral, and even more beautiful feline version of himself. The change was both physical and magical. He had the body of a god and was completely covered in shimmering golden fur. His hair grew into a crown that was part Afro and part lion's mane. His hands and feet turned into paws with sharp claws, and his clothes were torn and ripped at the seams. He definitely wasn't a werewolf. He was all man and all lion.

Zander tried to reach out to Tau but was stopped by Giovanni's bubble. Tau saw Zander reaching toward him and began to charge at the bubble with all of the ferocity of a hungry lion. Just as Tau reached the bubble, there was another loud boom. Zander's world went silent as a huge hunk of concrete started to fall from overhead. It was as if everything was in slow motion. Zander didn't know if Giovanni's bubble could withstand another blow, or if Tau was paying enough attention to the see the slab of concrete coming directly at him. Zander wanted to protect both of them. Zander looked over at Giovanni and watched him mouth the words, "Help me with this spell!" He turned and looked at Tau, who was still charging, and saw the ruby stone glowing around his neck with the intensity of a laser. The silence persisted for several more seconds before another boom was heard, and then Zander was thrown several feet across the room.

Exploding pellets whizzed through the air. The scent of club smoke and sweat was replaced by gun smoke and blood. Zander shook his head in an attempt to regain his composure. He began screaming for Giovanni and then Tau. Bodies and rubble lay strewn all around him. He searched his memory frantically for a spell that might offer protection or help him find his friends, but nothing came to mind. Despite his resolve, he began to cry. He tried to stand, and then realized that a large piece of metal had pierced his thigh.

"Zander, Get out of here!" someone yelled. Zander turned to find Milo the bartender backing toward him and casting spells at several advancing figures in uniform. Zander tried to make sense of it all. Milo was wielding significant amounts of earth magic, moving large volumes of air and throwing bolts of fire. Zander knew this kind of magic, and Milo was good at it. He turned and propped himself up on a leaning piece of wood just as a group of soldiers converged on one of the security guards and covered her like hyenas on a fresh kill.

"Get out!" Milo yelled again. Zander could see five men in full uniform and headgear pressing toward Milo. They were aiming their rifles at Milo and shooting something that resembled lightning. Zander took a deep breath and began calling up magic that sent tire-sized hunks of stone flying toward the soldiers. He took two of them out with the first slab of concrete, leaving Milo free to focus on the remaining three.

They were close enough now for Zander to hear one of the soldiers yell, "Set to kill. This one is dangerous!" So, they hadn't seen Zander. They assumed that all of the magic was coming from Milo. Zander had tried to help and had made things worse.

"No!" Zander yelled, and he reached out and took control of one of the fireballs that Milo had created and began reshaping it in midair. What had started out as a basketball-sized ball of fire from Milo now hung in the air and began to swirl and grow until it was the size of small automobile. Zander took it and hurled it at the three patrolmen. One dove out of the way. The remaining two weren't quite so lucky. The fire engulfed them, immediately burning through their uniforms and then their flesh. The first soldier tried unsuccessfully to run to put out the flames. The second fell to the floor after several seconds, and a large cloud of smoke escaped his lungs.

"Blessed be!" Milo yelled, helping Zander get to his feet.

"What is happening?" Zander cried, glad for Milo's assistance.

Milo didn't answer; instead he said, "We have to get out of here." Milo propped Zander up and helped him toward the numbered doors.

"Where are my friends?" Zander cried again. Milo didn't get a chance to answer. A bolt of lightning struck him square in the back, sending him and Zander tumbling to the ground. Zander smelled burnt flesh and turned to find a patrolman advancing toward him with his rifle raised. Milo's dead and burning body had Zander partially pinned to the ground. The soldier with the rifle was only a few feet away, with his weapon aimed right on Zander's chest.

Zander shut his eyes tight and waited for the lightning from the rifle to burn through his body. He wondered how long he would feel the pain and regretted the fact that he hadn't told his mother how much he loved her before he'd left home.

The pain didn't come. He opened his eyes and saw Tau spring out of nowhere and onto the unsuspecting soldier. Blood spewed everywhere as Tau pinned the soldier down and bit through his uniform and straight through his jugular. Tau turned toward Zander with a ferocity that made him shudder. Then he leapt across the room, gently moved and repositioned Milo's dead body, and cradled Zander with all the care of newborn. Zander didn't have time to object. Tau's was carrying him toward a large hole in the wall with inhuman speed. Zander took a gulp of fresh air as soon as they were outside. Witches, warlocks, shifters, and vampires were fighting soldiers outside the club, but the odds were different out here. The soldiers didn't have the element of surprise on their side, and the supernaturals ruled the night. Even equipped with night goggles, the soldiers were outmatched.

There was another loud boom, and the building behind them imploded. Fire trucks and police sirens could be heard off into the distance. Soldiers and supernaturals began disappearing into the night.

"We have to get out of here!" Tau yelled, with Zander

still in his arms. Zander kicked and protested.

"Giovanni is in there. I can't just leave him!" Zander yelled. Tau looked conflicted. He didn't like seeing Zander upset, but he knew that going back inside was nothing short of suicide. Zander tried to wrestle free, but he was unable to release himself from Tau's protective hold. The sirens grew closer, and the last few walls of Arcane crashed to the ground. Zander moaned and buried his head in Tau's chest, sobbing.

"We have to go," Tau whispered in his ear.

"Hey you big pussy! Put my friend down!"

"Giovanni!" Zander raised his head from Tau's chest in disbelief. Tau set Zander down so that he could embrace his friend.

"Now I know you weren't going to leave me," Giovanni teased.

"I am so sorry. I didn't know what to do. I'm so sorry." Zander sniffled.

"I could have used some help with the bubble. I see that I need to teach you a few force field spells," Giovanni said, punching Zander in the chest.

"I wish I could have done more," Zander admitted.

"I saw you back there helping Milo," Giovanni said. "You do know a few tricks."

"May his soul rest," Zander said, as was the customary saying when the name of any dead witch or warlock was mentioned.

"May he rest," Giovanni added.

"We need to go," Tau said again, urgently.

"Is your leg bleeding?" Giovanni asked Zander, already starting a healing spell.

"It's nothing. I'll be fine," Zander assured him.

"We have to leave now!" Tau growled at them.

"We know that!" Giovanni yelled back.

"My bike is on the other side of the building," Tau started.

"Your bike was crushed by the wall like all of the other bikes." Giovanni rolled his eyes. "Besides, Zander is in no shape to be on motorcycle, and there is no way that I am leaving him alone with you. Zander's car is just on the next street. We can take the back road to the highway." There was no more time to argue. Tau scooped Giovanni up in his right arm and Zander up in his left and began running in the direction of Zander's car. They were there within seconds. Tau threw Giovanni down on the ground and gently set Zander on the hood of the car.

"I have a spell that will make a nice fur coat out of you," Giovanni hissed, as he dusted himself off.

"I'll drive," Tau and Giovanni said in unison. The sirens drew closer.

"Let Giovanni drive. Tau, you can sit in the back with me," Zander suggested. Giovanni stuck his tongue out at Tau. Tau growled. They got into the car, where Zander quickly undid the protective spell over the glove compartment so that Giovanni could get the keys, and the car purred to life.

"Hurry up. We have to get away from here as quickly as possible," Tau barked from the backseat.

"Would you shut the fuck up? I know what I'm doing." Giovanni pulled out onto the street and headed back toward the highway.

"Where are you going?" Tau asked.

"We have to get somewhere safe. I'm headed back to my condo."

Zander reached up and put his hand over Tau's mouth before he could respond. Tau rolled his eyes and sighed, then looked out the window.

"You'd better change back," Giovanni told him. "We don't want to draw any extra attention. If the police see you sitting in the back seat, they'll think we stole an old lion from the zoo." Tau looked warily at Zander but didn't respond. Zander gave him a gentle kiss on the cheek. His fur was soft, like silk.

Tau's body began to convulse and change. Zander's head was against Tau's chest, and he was amazed as the soft fur changed back into flesh.

"I've never seen that up close before," Giovanni said, looking into the rearview mirror. "It's even nastier than I'd imagined." Tau stuck up his middle finger.

After his transformation, Tau laid his head back on the seat and took several deep breaths. Zander noticed the ruby stone that hung from Tau's neck lay cool against his chest.

Zander heard his phone ring from the glove compartment. "Shit! That has to be my family. My cousins probably can't find me at the Litha, and my parents are probably worried sick. They have no idea where I am."

"You know..." Giovanni mused. "I was just thinking about something. Who did you say gave you that ruby stone that you gave to the Pink Panther?"

"Give me my phone," Zander said, ignoring Giovanni's question.

Zander had several missed calls from his parents, cousins, and grandmother. He took a second to send them all a text saying that he was fine and resting in his tent at the Litha.

Tau's head was back on the headrest, and his eyes were closed. Zander's head lay on Tau's chest, as he listened to his labored breathing. The transformation must have taken a greater toll on Tau than Zander had imagined. His phone vibrated in his hand, indicating an incoming call from his parents. He leaned forward, suffering through the stabbing pain in his leg as he answered the call with a whisper.

"Zander!" his father yelled.

"Yes?" Zander whispered.

"Are you okay? We've gotten word of an attack on supernaturals in the Atlanta area. Your cousins at the Litha can't seem to find you anywhere. Where are you?"

"I was asleep," Zander said, trying to sound drowsy. Giovanni was nearing his condo in Atlantic Station.

"I don't think you understand..." his father started. Zander cast a small interference spell on the phone.

"Dad, I think I'm losing the connection," Zander lied.

"No!" his father yelled, right before Zander hung up the phone.

They pulled up to the large basement garage at Giovanni's condo, where he entered his code to open one of the single garage doors. Tau rose up in the back seat and began sniffing the air.

"Don't worry. It's safe here," Giovanni said. "I have protective charms all around this building."

"I'm sure they had protective charms all around the club tonight, and you saw what happened," Tau said.

"I didn't invoke those charms," Giovanni pointed out.

"No, you were too busy letting all the vampires in the club suck all over you," Tau said.

"Stop it!" Zander yelled. "You two arguing isn't helping."

Giovanni sighed and pulled into one of the parking spaces designated for his condo and turned off the car. "I live in 706. There are eight cameras in this garage, so no shifting unless it is absolutely necessary. Let's get out and go up to my place like everything's normal."

"I don't know if I can walk on my own," Zander said.

"Suck it up until you get to the elevator," Giovanni ordered. "We'll walk slowly. We don't want to draw any extra attention."

They made it up to Giovanni's place without incident, and before Giovanni unlocked the door, he looked up and down the hallway and quietly chanted an incantation.

He waited several seconds before turning the key and entering his apartment.

The apartment was beautifully decorated with plush furniture in various shades of gray and burgundy. Not surprisingly, it smelled of sandalwood and lavender. Magic and arcane symbols were displayed throughout the condominium like works of art. Zander wasn't sure why, but he hadn't expected Giovanni's place to be so neatly organized. Giovanni snapped his fingers, magically lighting each of the candles in his apartment with witch light.

"Someone is here," Tau warned.

"Relax, Tony the Tiger. It's Hung." Giovanni pointed as the vampire from the club came out of his bedroom completely nude with a rock hard erection.

"I've been waiting for you," Hung said, ignoring Zander and Tau.

"I was scared that you might not have gotten out in time," Giovanni said, giving Hung a hug.

"What do you mean? What happened?"

"I'll be there in a moment to explain it all to you. Just go back to bed and wait for me. I have something to attend to." Giovanni pushed Hung back toward the bedroom.

"I need you now," Hung whined, stroking his sizable cock and forcing precome to the tip. Giovanni exposed the fresh bite wound on his neck, pinched out a drop of blood onto his finger, and gently placed it on Hung's lips.

"You'll have all of me if you're patient. I just need a few minutes to take care of my friend," Giovanni said. Hung licked and sucked the blood from Giovanni's finger like a baby nursing on a bottle. Once he was mildly sated, he turned to walk off toward the bedroom as Giovanni had instructed. Zander couldn't help but notice that Hung had the perky ass of a gymnast. Tau growled again. Once

Hung had wandered back into the bedroom, Giovanni locked the door behind him and cast a small binding spell on the door.

"I don't have a lot of time. Zander, take off your clothes and come with me." Giovanni reached for Zander's hand.

Tau grabbed Zander's other hand. "What do you think you're doing?"

"Relax, Lion-O. I'm not trying to steal your man. His wounds need to be tended to, and last time I checked, you weren't a healer." Giovanni rolled his eyes.

"We shifters have our own methods of healing," Tau responded.

"We don't have time for your ancient shifting medicine man antics. A cleansing bath and a few healing spells, and he'll be good as new. You do want him healed, don't you?" Giovanni asked.

"Be careful, and don't take too long," Tau warned.

"First, you don't threaten me in my house," Giovanni said hotly. "Second, I have a nice piece of dick waiting for me in my bedroom. I am going to do this as quickly as possible. Now take your tired furry ass into the guest bedroom and lie down."

Giovanni drug Zander off toward the bathroom where he quickly drew a hot bath and added several salts and herbs. Once Zander was undressed and in the bath, Giovanni cast three different healing spells over his injured thigh.

"That feels great. Thank you. You really are a good friend," Zander admitted.

"The best you'll ever have." Giovanni smiled.

"You are so smart." Zander watched in amazement as the gash on his thigh rapidly began to heal.

Giovanni smiled back. "Necessity is the mother of invention. I've had to learn a lot of street magic in order to survive. What they teach in school is useful, but there is so much more to learn." While Zander soaked, Giovanni pulled out a small paper cup and started mixing a potion from ingredients in his medicine cabinet. It didn't take long for the contents of the cup to start bubbling and smoking. "Sit up and drink this."

"What is it?" Zander asked, warily.

"It's a special concoction. It'll relax you, which will help with the healing and other things," Giovanni said coyly.

"Other things like what?" Zander asked suspiciously.

"You trust me, don't you?" Giovanni asked.

"Yes." Zander sighed and swallowed. When he finished, Giovanni took the cup and made it disappear into thin air.

"What the hell do you think happened in the club tonight?" Zander asked.

"Damn if I know, but it sure as hell wasn't expected. I thought it was a part of the club's entertainment at first."

"I'm sorry about Milo," Zander said sadly. "I wish I could have saved him."

"He was a good warlock. I saw his magic. He died in the light. Good things await him," Giovanni assured Zander.

"So, what do we do now?" Zander asked.

"I am sure the supernatural grapevine will be on fire in the morning when we wake up," Giovanni said. "We'll find out then. In the meantime, we need to stay here out of harm's way. It might have been one of the newer supernatural gangs trying to make a name for themselves."

"There are supernatural gangs?"

"You really do have a lot to learn." Giovanni laughed, shedding his clothes.

"What are you doing?" Zander asked.

"I have a man waiting for me, too, and there is nothing

sexier than a ripening warlock dipped in a tantric mating bath," Giovanni said.

It felt good having Giovanni wash his body. He knew that Tau wouldn't approve, but Giovanni wasn't making any sexual gestures. He was caring for Zander in a way that he had never experienced before. Zander returned the favor by washing Giovanni's tight, tawny body. When they were finished, they dried each other off slowly, forcing their individual scents to mingle.

"You know our scents smell really good together. Hung and Cheetara aren't going to know what hit them," Giovanni said.

"Why do you have to tease him? You know it makes him angry. Why can't you call him by his name?"

"Because he's so damn uptight. He needs to relax." Giovanni retrieved two outfits from the bathroom closet and threw Zander a pair of red silk boxers with a matching shirt. "We're the same size. These should fit you perfectly."

Zander slipped on the sexy outfit and glanced in the mirror. "How do I look?"

"You look okay. Your flat ass doesn't fill out the shorts as well as mine does, but that's to be expected," Giovanni joked.

"Fuck you." Zander said, giving his own ass a slap while he admired it in the mirror.

Tau was pacing back and forth in the hallway when Zander finally opened the bathroom door.

"Aren't you just a little anxious?" Giovanni snapped at Tau.

"No, Geronimo. I was anxious over an hour ago. I am flat-out impatient now," Tau retorted.

"Zander isn't one of those alley cats that you're used to fucking. This is a ripe, virgin warlock." Giovanni stepped aside to reveal a rather shy Zander. Tau was speechless.

"What's wrong? Cat got your tongue?" Giovanni asked, grinning.

"Giovanni! I am locked in here. I think the door is stuck!" It sounded like Hung was banging on the door to the master bedroom.

"I have work to do," Giovanni said. "You two can help yourself to the guest bedroom." He gave Zander a quick hug and rushed off to his own bedroom.

"You look so... good. You smell great. Do you think your friend will mind if I take a shower?" Tau asked Zander.

"Go ahead!" Giovanni yelled from his bedroom. "There are towels and washcloths in the closet!" The door slammed shut.

"I'll just go lie down," Zander said, as he tried to put the evening's events into perspective. He was in a strange house about to go to bed with someone he had only met a few hours ago, he had just seen a club attacked and burned to the ground by soldiers, and here he was prancing around in sexy lingerie. His apprehensions melted away when Tau reached down and gave him a soft kiss on the lips.

"I'll be out before you know it," Tau murmured, before closing the bathroom door.

Giovanni's guest bedroom was beautiful, and a large bed lay just a few inches above the floor, covered in dozens of pillows. The witch light in the room reminded Zander of home. His mother had used witch light when he was a toddler to help him fall asleep. He eased down onto the bed and realized that it was the most comfortable mattress that he had ever felt. It dawned on him that he had been sleeping on the same twin-sized bed since he was seven years old.

It was time that he grew up. He lay on his stomach and buried his face into the mountain of pillows. The silk pajamas, brushed cotton sheets, and cool pillows felt like heaven. It wasn't long before Zander was asleep and drooling.

Chapter 6

When Zander woke up, Tau was laying propped up on his side, staring. Zander could only imagine how unattractive he must have looked drooling and snoring in his sleep.

"How long have I been asleep?" Zander asked.

"Not too long." Tau rubbed his back.

"Why didn't you wake me?"

"Because I enjoy watching you sleep. You've been through a lot. I figured you needed the rest."

"Thank you—I think. I see you showered," Zander said, noticing that Tau was totally clean and completely naked. His flaccid dick hung from his midsection and lay across the bed like a sleeping serpent.

Tau grinned. "Do you see something you like?"

"Maybe," Zander said, sounding more seductive than he intended. He had never been with anyone, let alone a man as well endowed as Tau.

"I certainly see a few things that I like," Tau responded.

"Let me guess—my booty, right?"

"That is nice, too, but I was referring to your lips." Tau gave Zander a soft and passionate peck on his lips. One peck turned into a few more, and the pecks turned into full kisses. Zander rolled up on top of Tau and began grinding his hips. Tau slid his large hands down inside

Giovanni's red silk shorts and grabbed his ass.

"Your skin is so smooth and soft," Tau remarked, but Zander couldn't respond. He was ripening; he was naturally attracted to Tau, but Zander suspected that Giovanni's potion had been an aphrodisiac. He had never felt so horny and out of control. His dick was as hard as a rock, and his ass was beginning to self-lubricate. Like most gay warlocks, Zander's body had evolved to accommodate gay sex by secreting a sweet, clear liquid whenever he was highly aroused. Tau's dick was stiffening as well, and it looked to be as long as Zander's forearm by the time Zander started sucking his nipples. Tau's low groan turned into a moan as Zander made his way down toward Tau's abdomen with soft kisses.

"You feel so damn good," Tau huffed. Zander was insatiable. He pushed Tau back onto the bed and turned around so that his fat, round ass was directly in Tau's face. Then he began licking Tau's big dick like a kid licking a popsicle in the middle of summer. Zander had secretly paid attention when his high school cheerleader girlfriends talked about sucking the big dicks of the local football stars. He had even practiced in the privacy of his own room with bananas and then larger cucumbers. The cheerleaders talked about the most sensitive parts of the penis and how to stimulate each of them. Zander found that he enjoyed the feel of Tau's dick in the mouth.

Tau responded by literally ripping the red silk shorts off of Zander. The aggressive move turned Zander on even more, and he opened his throat and took as much of Tau's dick as he could. Tau growled and punched a hole in the headboard. Zander's scent filled the room, acting as an aphrodisiac on Tau. Zander continued licking Tau's huge, weighty balls and then his muscular inner thighs. Tau couldn't take it any longer. He sprang up from the bed and flipped Zander onto his stomach. Zander's fat, round ass sat up in the air like a piece of ripe fruit. Tau buried his face in Zander's ass and began to swirl his tongue inside him until Zander trembled.

"You feel so good," Zander panted.

"You're so wet, and you taste so damn good," Tau said in between slurps.

Zander looked behind him and whispered, "I want you." Tau's dick appeared even larger as the vein that ran along the top of his dick started to throb, and precome oozed from the tip of it. Tau flipped Zander over onto his back, pushed his legs open and straddled him. Zander responded by pulling his ankles up by his head. He was practically bent in half, wide open for Tau. Tau smiled in appreciation. Zander grabbed Tau's dick and pulled it toward his ripe hole. Even Zander's hand looked small next to Tau's large penis.

"If you take it slow, then it might not hurt so much in the morning," Tau said, grinning. Zander responded by seductively licking his middle finger and then sliding it inside his wet hole. Tau grabbed his shaft and slowly guided it toward Zander's waiting hole. Zander sighed when Tau's fat dick head pressed against him. Tau massaged Zander's hole with the head of his dick, using his precome for lubrication. Zander threw his head back and thrust his ass up toward Tau's dick.

Tau pulled back, sat up for a moment, and then buried his face in Zander's crotch, where he started to lick his balls, suck his hole, and slurp on his dick. Zander rocked his hips to accommodate Tau.

"May I have you?" Tau asked, his voice trembling.

"Please!" Zander chanted a small spell that made the witch light in the room swirl, go dim, and then change colors from brown to red to orange.

Zander braced himself, arched his back, and took a deep breath when Tau pushed that enormous dick head inside him. The precome from Tau's dick and the moisture from Zander's dripping hot ass helped with the entry, but Tau had a dick with an unusually thick head that only got thicker with every inch. Tau only had the head of his dick in Zander when Zander's eyes began to water and his breaths became shallow.

"Relax," Tau said softly. Zander wrapped his arms around Tau's neck, pulled him into a loving embrace, and then gave him another passionate kiss. Tau eased another inch of dick into Zander, forcing Tau to accidentally bite his lip.

"I'm sorry," Zander said, as the blood from Tau's lip dripped into his mouth.

"Should I... stop?" Tau asked, hesitantly. Zander didn't respond. He simply pushed his hips further onto Tau, accepting a little bit more. Tau began to rock his hips gently, pulling out to the tip and then sliding back in just a little bit further each time.

When he had about half of his dick inside Zander, Zander asked naively, "Is it all the way in?"

Tau smiled and said, "Not yet, baby." A tear rolled from Zander's eye.

"What's wrong?" Tau asked.

"Nothing. Do I feel good to you?" Zander asked.

"You feel great." Tau placed several kisses all over Zander's face. Zander exhaled, and his hole opened up a little further, accepting yet another inch of Tau's dick. Tau moaned in ecstasy. More of his warm precome leaked out inside of Zander, and they both sighed. The more Tau pressed in, the wetter Zander became. As Tau rocked slowly inside Zander, their bodies began to make a sweet gushing sound that nearly made Tau lose control.

In a surprise move, Zander wrapped his legs around Tau's waist and thrust his hips, taking several more inches. Tau roared. The ruby that Zander had given him swung back and forth like a pendulum, hitting Zander in the face with each stroke. Zander saw white lights as his mind tried to register the difference between pleasure and pain.

Zander's scent, tight wet hole, and raw passion were more than Tau could stand. Tau's slow rocking movements turned into quick pelvic thrusts. Before he knew it, he was slamming into Zander's virgin hole. Zander bit his lip and held onto Tau for dear life. The pain eventually turned to pressure, and the pressure eventually turned to pleasure. While Tau was banging into Zander, Zander shot a huge load of come. His orgasm coated both their stomachs, adding an even stronger sexual scent to the air.

Tau roared, and then it happened—he began to transform. Zander didn't know what to do. Tau was changing and growing, and his dick was getting larger while he was still inside him. As Tau reached the peak of his transformation, he ejaculated inside Zander, sending a jolt of primal magic through Zander's entire body. The result was an explosion of light and energy that sent Tau flying across the room and Zander shivering in ecstasy.

Chapter 7

iovanni! Help!"

When Giovanni and Hung rushed into the guest bedroom wrapped up in nothing but sheets, Tau was sprawled out on the floor, naked and still unconscious. Zander was curled up in the bed screaming.

"Bitch, What in the fuck is wrong with you?" Giovanni yelled.

"I think I killed him," Zander wept.

"Were you fucking?" Giovanni asked.

"Well, yes."

"Did he come?" Giovanni continued.

"Well, yes."

"Did he come inside of you?" Giovanni asked, impatiently.

"Yes," Zander responded, looking shyly at Hung. Giovanni and Hung burst out into laughter.

"Why are you laughing?" Zander asked, as Hung repositioned Tau on the floor and covered him with a stray sheet.

"He will be fine. You probably just gave him the best orgasm of his life," Giovanni explained.

"That's for sure," Hung said, giving Giovanni a hug from behind.

"What do you mean?" Zander asked.

"Shifting is high magic. When shifters are really aroused during sex, they can sometimes begin to transform if they aren't careful. If you two were being intimate and you were that close to that much powerful magic, then your body probably just reacted—especially since you were a virgin," Giovanni said.

"You gave him your cherry?" Hung asked, eyebrows raised high.

Zander hung his head. "This is so damn embarrassing."

"Yes, and from the looks of things in this room, he must have done a pretty good job of giving him the cherry. My headboard has a hole in it, the bed is torn up, and the room smells like good sex. Here, kitty, kitty." Giovanni gave three snaps and a circle over Tau's unconscious body.

"I'm sorry. I'll pay to get everything fixed," Zander offered.

"Is that a witch's ruby looking stone?" Hung asked.

"Shit!" Giovanni said.

"What's wrong now?" Zander went to Tau's side and cradled his head in his lap.

"I meant to explain that to you earlier." Giovanni winced. "With everything going on, I completely forgot! If that is a really a looking stone—and I think it is— whoever it gave it to you is probably able to see you."

"What? My grandmother gave me that!" Zander screamed. Hung burst out into laughter again.

"Is she a powerful witch?" Giovanni asked.

"Yes, why?" Zander countered.

Hung's cell phone rang from the other room. "This is priceless. I haven't laughed so hard in my life. Video his reaction when you explain it to him," Hung said as he left the room.

Giovanni sighed. "A powerful witch or warlock can take a precious stone—like a diamond, ruby, emerald— and create a kind of looking glass. You see, they can enchant a large stone, magically break off a portion of it, and then use the large stone to see through the smaller stone. It's kind of like..."

"Oh my god! You mean my grandmother saw everything that happened?" Zander buried his face in his hands.

Tau moaned softly.

Zander kissed Tau's cradled forehead. "Are you all right?"

"Damn, baby!" Tau smiled. "That was fantastic."

Giovanni smirked. "I bet it was."

"What's Juju Bee doing in here?" Tau asked, glaring at Giovanni.

"Magic has already fucked you up once tonight," Giovanni warned.

Hung came rushing back into the bedroom. "This shit is serious! Last night wasn't just some random act of supernatural gang violence. Not only did Club Arcane get hit, but some people are saying that humans might even have been responsible!"

"Shit!" Zander, Giovanni, and Tau responded in unison.

"How do you know?" Giovanni asked Hung.

"My house sister called. She has been trying to reach me since last night, but I guess I was... a little bit preoccupied."

"How could it be humans?" Giovanni wondered aloud. "Most of them don't even believe that we exist."

"This is too much. I probably need to head home," Zander started.

"It's no big deal. Just take your boy home with you and tell them you are mated now. They'll understand." Hung shrugged.

"What?" Zander asked.

"Giovanni told me that you two exchanged family

gifts last night," Hung said. "And it's obvious that you consummated the relationship. Isn't that how shifters marry and mate?"

"*What?*" Zander asked again.

Hung rolled his eyes. "You say 'what' an awful lot."

"Mated?" Zander stood up, letting Tau's head drop to the floor.

Hung continued, "Shifters mate for life and typically have little to no courtship. I guess they just know when they find the right one. Isn't that right, Tau?"

Zander gaped at Tau. "You tried to trick me into a mating ceremony without telling me?"

"I...I...I...," Tau stuttered.

Zander turned on Giovanni. "And did you know he was *mating* with me?"

"I thought you knew." Giovanni shrugged. "You used to tell me that all you ever wanted was a love of your own."

"Baby, let me explain," Tau said, standing and wrapping himself in the sheet.

"This shit is crazy!" Zander yelled. "I had sex for the first time last night and knocked my lover unconscious. Then I find out that he was trying to marry me on the low, and my grandmother probably watched the whole thing on some supernatural video stone!"

Hung continued, "I think you had better sit down. There is more. My house sister says that there were more victims. They also attacked a coven of vampires in Lithonia, a pack of shifters in College Park... the Litha, and a caravan of witches driving into Atlanta."

Zander dropped to his knees. "My family."

Chapter 8

Zander couldn't reach any of his family members by phone, and he was inconsolable and hysterical. "Just relax." Giovanni patted his shoulder. "We can figure this out. I'm sure that your family is all right."

"Yes, baby," Tau added as he wrapped the bed sheet around his body like a toga. "Just take a deep breath. We'll figure this out."

"Motherfucker, you don't get to call me *baby*. You lied to me!" Zander yelled.

"Uh oh." Hung raised his eyebrows.

"Zander, what are you talking about?" Tau asked, sounding hurt. "I know you feel the chemistry between us. We are right together. Maybe, I should—"

Before he could finish, Zander waved his arms through the air and sent Tau flying into the wall. The result was a stunned Tau and a large hole in Giovanni's guest bedroom wall.

"I bet that hurt," Hung commented.

"I trusted you!" Zander screamed. "I gave you my whole name, my grandmother's necklace, and my body, and then you lied to me!"

"The neighbors will hear," Giovanni warned. "Take it done a notch."

Zander made a quick gesture with his hand, and the leather strap of the necklace that he had given to Tau began twisting and tightening around Tau's neck.

"Zander, stop!" Giovanni yelled. Tau pulled at the necklace to try keep it from strangling him, but Zander's magic was just too strong. Hung dashed across the room and slashed at the necklace several times with his razor sharp nails, finally cutting the cord—and Tau's neck several times in the process. The ruby and its leather cord fell to the floor. Tau reached for it despite the fact that blood was pouring from his neck, but Zander was too quick. He made another slight gesture with his left hand, and the ruby flew across the room and right into Zander's palm.

"But that gift acknowledges our bond," Tau said, as if he couldn't begin to understand Zander's anger.

"There is no bond. You are a liar," Zander replied coolly, as he stomped off toward the bathroom to get dressed.

"I'm sorry that I cut you," Hung said to Tau, looking at the blood spilling from his neck.

"How about you stop checking his neck out like that?" Giovanni scolded Hung, sounding more like a jealous boyfriend than actually concerned for Tau's safety.

"You were only trying to help," Tau told Hung.

"I think you two had better leave. This is magical business, and I need to help Zander work through this," Giovanni said.

"Leave now? The sun is up, and I'm a vampire, remember? I don't do sunlight. And I thought you said we were going to have sex all day." Hung pouted. "Why have I got to leave? He's the one that lied." He pointed over at Tau.

"This is serious," Giovanni explained. "Zander has never been away from home, and he can't find his family.

He's out of control, and there's no telling what he might do. I need to calm him down."

"I should be the one to help him," Tau said, sulking a little.

"Look, Calvin and Hobbes, *you* found your soul mate and started the shifter mating process last night, but *Zander* feels like he got fucked and lied to last night. I'm sure that you are a great guy..." Giovanni snorted as he cast a spell over the cuts on Tau's neck to speed the healing. "But there are still a lot of things about the supernatural world that Zander doesn't understand."

"So, now why do *I* have to leave?" Hung asked again.

Giovanni sighed. "I have to help Zander. He barely knows how to use his magic, and he's an emotional wreck right now. A warlock's magic is directly tied to his feelings. He needs me right now. You can have me later. Now go get dressed."

Hung eased over to Giovanni like he owned him, grabbed him by his hips, and pulled him close. Then, with all of the practice and natural seduction of a vampire, he leaned in and pricked Giovanni's neck with his right canine tooth and lapped several sips of blood. When Hung had satisfied his thirst, he walked out of the room without so much as a word. Giovanni swooned.

"As nasty as that was, it is obvious that you two were made for each other," Tau commented.

"Look Simba, you need to stay out of my business and worry about your own man problems," Giovanni snapped.

"I hate to admit it, but you're right. How can Zander not see what *we* have? Maybe I should have taken things slower and told him about my intent to mate, but I know he's the one. We shifters mate on instinct. I know that is was more than fate that guided us to the same place at the same time. It was something more primal than that.

I sensed him as soon as I walked in the club. Everything about Zander feels right to me." Tau picked up the sheets from the floor in a feeble attempt to straighten up the destroyed guest bedroom.

"I'm sure that he feels it. It's pretty obvious that you two have... a thing." Giovanni smiled wryly. "This is all just a lot for him to take in right now. His family has to be his priority. Maybe he'll feel differently after he calms down. In the meantime, he probably needs to keep the ruby to help him try to find his family. And don't worry about the room. I'll fix it later."

"I'm sorry about the headboard and the wall," Tau said sincerely.

Giovanni rolled his eyes. "Just go get dressed."

"I left my clothes in the bathroom, and I think Zander is still in there," Tau whispered. "I don't think he is ready to see me yet."

"Yeah, right. I'll go get your clothes for you. You had the polyester shirt and JC Penney jeans, right?"

They both laughed.

"Hey, Ginger Snap," Tau said, before Giovanni exited the room.

"Yes, Panthro?"

"Thank you," Tau said, bowing his head.

"Don't mention it. Just don't leave any fur balls in my bedroom."

Tau paced back and forth in Giovanni's guest bedroom like the lion that he was.

"Dammit!" Giovanni yelled from the living room. Hung and Tau raced into the bathroom.

"What is it?" they asked in unison.

"Zander's gone!"

Chapter 9

Despite the fact that magic came easier to Zander when he was angry, leaving Giovanni's condominium under the cover of a cloaking spell had been much more difficult than throwing Tau across the room. Tears welled up in Zander's eyes as he remembered the look on Tau's face when he took the ruby stone back. He kept telling himself that Tau had lied to him and that Tau had gotten exactly what he deserved, but being separated was breaking Zander's heart.

His thoughts drifted from Tau to his family, and then the tears began to flow. His family had to be fine. Worst case, they would be mad at him for lying and ground him. He picked up his phone from the passenger seat and dialed each of their cell numbers. Neither his father, mother, aunts, uncles, nor cousins answered their phones. He dialed his Grandmother Zoe last. She always answered before the first ring—she had to. By the time her phone rang the seventh time, Zander was bawling.

What would have normally been a four and a half hour drive from Atlanta to Zander's home in one of the southernmost towns in Georgia, only took three and a half hours driving at seventy miles per hour. He wondered if they had any idea that he had left the Litha. He wondered why they weren't answering the phone. He wondered if it was his family's caravan that had been attacked on the way to Atlanta.

"Think positive, think positive," he told himself, but that didn't console him.

He remembered the time that his Grandmother Zoe morphed into a replica of his Grandmother Nasha and did the Stanky Legg dance in the front yard, and he burst out laughing through his tears. She would call him back any minute—she had to.

When Zander zoomed by one of the speed traps that southerners always warned their northern relatives about, a police car pulled out after him with lights flashing and sirens blaring.

"I really don't have time for this shit right now," he mumbled, and turned his wrist several times, instantly flattening all four of the officer's tires.

As he gripped the steering wheel, he looked down at the ring finger on his right hand, saw the ring that Tau had given him, and immediately remembered everything—especially the sex. It was amazing. He was sore in muscles that he didn't know he had, his legs had just stopped trembling, and his ass was still humming. It didn't matter now. He had probably blown any chance of ever seeing Tau again after his little temper tantrum. It occurred to him that Tau could have defended himself; Tau could have shifted and attacked him, but he didn't. Instead, he looked as if his heart had been ripped from his chest. The tears came again.

Zander glanced over at his phone. No one had called. "Dammit!"

It was as much of an emotional roller coaster for Zander as it was a race home to find his family. He was sixty miles out when he started to get angry for not having been given the magical training that was his birthright. He knew that his parents loved him, but he was starting to think that they had made a critical error in judgment in raising him in the ways of mortals.

He would be home right at high noon, which was when his mother normally steeped her love potions for maximum potency. His father would be at his computer obsessing over fluctuations in the stock market or looking for ways to magically influence local political races without being noticed. Like all magicals, Zander's parents' only job was to stay beyond the suspicion of any nearby mortals and appear as "normal" as possible. Most magical families had secured significant wealth several generations ago through the use of magic and just busied themselves with what most mortals would consider trivial pursuits, socializing and traveling abroad. When Zander's friends asked what his parents did for a living, he would lie and say that his father was a day trader who worked from home and his mother was an art buyer for wealthy investors.

His phone rang, and he grabbed it from the passenger's seat immediately. It was Giovanni. Zander was too embarrassed to talk to him. After all of Giovanni's hospitality, Zander had torn up his guest bedroom, thrown a fit, and stormed out without even saying goodbye.

There was no wonder his cousins treated him the way they did, especially that damn Waverly Knight, his Uncle Siran's oldest son. Waverly was his older first cousin on his father's side. Zander had always sought Waverly's approval—even imagined that he was the big brother that Zander never had—but Waverly was typically dismissive and sometimes downright mean. Waverly was everything a warlock was supposed to be—cool, confident, cultured. It had been Waverly who was given responsibility for introducing Zander to the available young witches at the Litha... and now he could possibly be dead.

His phone rang for the sixth time before he decided

to let it simply go to voicemail. What could he say to fix things with Giovanni at this point? Not only had he managed to lose a great guy in Tau, he had also probably alienated the closest thing that he'd ever had to a warlock best friend.

The closer he got to his house, the more nervous he became. He turned onto the highway that led to his house. He had grown accustomed to the quiet solitude that his family's large, country estate provided. Friends were invited over only during times of low magical significance, which left very little opportunity when you considered the various solstice and equinox periods and all of the necessary wiccan activities that led up to them. His phone rang again. It was Giovanni. He didn't answer—he couldn't.

Chapter 10

How could he get out without you hearing him?" Tau snarled.

"What are you trying to say?" Giovanni asked, eyebrows raised.

"You knew he was upset. Was it too hard for you to keep an eye on him? Was that just too much responsibility for you?"

"Let's not forget that you are part of the reason that he got so upset in the first fucking place," Giovanni spit.

"I knew you were a damn mess when I first met you." Tau pulled his large hands through his hair, obviously frustrated.

"You've already been thrown into one wall by a warlock this morning," Giovanni reminded him. "Let's not make it two... or three. If I get started slinging your ass around this room, I just might not stop."

"I'd choke the shit out of you before you could even get started," Tau hissed.

"Stop!" Hung yelled. "This arguing isn't doing any good. You both want the same thing."

Giovanni and Tau went to their mutual corners, never taking their eyes off of one another.

"You both should go get dressed," Hung said, palms raised. "I'll fix you something to eat, and then we can figure out what to do next."

Giovanni softened. Not only was Hung a good fuck, but he seemed like a good guy, too. Giovanni was the last person on earth to be looking for love or anything close to it. Everyone that he had ever cared about had let him down, and he wasn't keen on getting too attached to anyone too soon. It had taken months and months of online chatting with Zander for Giovanni to begin to trust him. Giovanni did a good job of acting as if he didn't care about most people or things, but he did care. He wasn't sure what Hung wanted, but Giovanni would keep his eyes open until he found out.

Tau headed off to the guest bathroom while Giovanni went to his master suite yapping all the way.

"There's fruit in the refrigerator and granola and honey in the pantry," he called. "Just throw it all in a bowl for me. If you can find some rancid meat in the back of the fridge, you can give that to Tau."

Tau rolled his eyes. "I see that you know your way around the kitchen." He propped himself against the kitchen island.

"You could say that." Hung handed the plated raw steak over to Tau. "When you've lived as long as I have, you tend to get pretty good at quite a few things. I've actually studied at the Academia Barilla and the Lenotre."

"You're pretty lucky to have lived along enough to attend two of the best culinary schools in the world."

"I see you know something about world travel and culinary schools," Hung said with a smile.

"A little," Tau admitted, looking around the kitchen for a utensil. Hung found the utensil drawer and tossed him a knife and a fork.

"Speaking of luck, it looks like we both got pretty lucky last night, huh?" Hung winked.

Tau sighed. "I don't know about how lucky we are. I

seem to have lost Zander, and you are dating the devil."

Hung laughed. "Gio isn't that bad. I like the fact that he is full of contradictions. He tries to act all hard and callous, but you can see from his concern for Zander that he is really a sweetheart. And don't get me started on his sex game... crazy!"

They both burst out laughing and gave each other high fives.

"What the fuck is this?" Giovanni said, idling into the kitchen.

"Tau was thanking me for the steak," Hung said solemnly. Tau snickered.

"Uh huh," Giovanni said.

"This is for you," Hung said, offering Giovanni his granola, fruit, and honey breakfast. Giovanni rolled his eyes and accepted a kiss on the cheek from Hung. Tau and Giovanni ate in relative silence while Hung straightened up the kitchen. Hung gave Tau a smile and a wink while Giovanni wasn't looking.

Tau cleared his throat. "So what's the plan?"

"I have to go find Zander," Giovanni announced.

"I'm going with you," Tau declared.

"No, you are not," Giovanni sang.

"Where do you think he went?" Hung asked.

"Home. It's the only logical place for him to go," Giovanni smacked through mouthfuls of granola, while repeatedly dialing Zander's mobile phone.

"So you know where he lives? You've been to his house?" Hung asked.

"Not exactly," Giovanni said.

"So what are you going to do?" Hung asked.

"I don't know. I could cast a locater spell to track him if I had something that belonged to him, but he took all of his things with him when he left. He didn't even leave a sock or a funky pair of drawers," Giovanni huffed.

"So how does this locater spell thing work?" Tau asked, wiping the steak juice from his chin and licking his lips.

Giovanni sighed. "I basically take something that belongs to him, magically attach it to a divining rod made of some type of untreated wood, mahogany is best, and use it to guide me to him like two halves of a magnet. I don't know why I am even explaining this to you. I can't really expect you to understand this type of complex magic."

"So, does it work the other way around?" Tau asked.

"What do you mean, Wilykat?" Giovanni asked, setting his granola down on the kitchen island.

"Zander still had on the ring that I gave him when he ran out of the bedroom. If he still has it on, can we use your magic divining rod idea to take me to the ring?"

Giovanni smiled reluctantly, tilted his head, and scratched his chin. "It may work. It depends on whether or not he has completely accepted the ring as his or if he still considers it yours. You owned the ring longer, so it could still have your aural signature on it."

"Which means you have to take me with you," Tau announced.

"So if Zander hasn't accepted the ring and Tau as his mate, then you can use the ring to find him?" Hung asked.

"Basically," Giovanni answered.

"That is kind of a fucked up way to find out that he isn't digging you," Hung added.

"But if I can find him, then maybe I can talk to him," Tau said.

"Once again, Wilykat, this isn't about you. This is about Zander. We still don't know what happened to his family. He could be driving right into the same danger that attacked the club last night," Giovanni said.

"We have to leave now," Tau said with urgency. "I just need my bike."

"Your motorcycle was probably crushed by the wall when the building fell," Giovanni reminded him.

Hung glanced over at Tau. "Do you think the people who attacked the club could possibly trace your bike back to you or someone in your family?"

Tau snorted. "We shifters aren't that stupid. We try to live outside the grid as much as possible. My tags were faked, and the bike was purchased on the black market. They'll never find me or any member of my family."

"What if he threw the ring out of the window on the highway?" Hung asked, thoughtful.

"Would you just stop with the negativity?" Tau asked.

Giovanni sighed. "So now what do we do?"

"You can take my car," Hung said, sending a text on his phone. "I'll have one of the help bring it to you right now. I'll stay here until the sun goes down, and then I'll come find you."

Giovanni wasn't sure that he wanted Hung to stay in his house alone or get in the habit of coming to find him every time the sun went down, but what choice did he have? He needed to use Hung's car, and he couldn't exactly put a vampire out in the daytime, could he?

"Okay, then. Hung, we'll use your car. Tigger, go get your shit, and let's go. Like every good warlock, I have a divining rod already carved. I'll just need something that belongs to you to connect with the ring. The more personal it is, the better."

Giovanni turned to Hung and ran down a list of things that Hung could not do in his condo, which included inviting over any other male guests, answering his phone, or looking in his bottom nightstand drawer.

Hung just laughed and kept running his fingers through Giovanni's dreadlocks. "Go get your stuff. I'll straighten up while you are gone," Hung said, patting him lightly on the ass.

There were all back in the living room within minutes. Giovanni was holding a wooden, Y-shaped instrument about the size of coat hanger.

"You warlocks and your toys," Tau laughed.

"You didn't mind the warlock's toys last night," Giovanni snapped. Tau rolled his eyes and cleared his throat.

"Me either," Hung interjected.

"So, what do you need for the divining rod thing?" Tau asked Giovanni.

"Something personal that is closely attached to you or the ring that you gave to Zander."

"The cowrie shell was in my hair—how about a piece of my hair?"

"That should work," Giovanni said. Hung rushed off to get a pair of scissors that he had seen in Giovanni's potions cabinet. When he returned, Tau obliged Giovanni by tilting his head. Giovanni grabbed an ample handful of Tau's hair, tugged at it for good measure, and then cut several inches from the root at the very front of Tau's head.

"Did you really need that much fucking hair?" Tau asked incredulously.

"You want to find him, don't you?" Giovanni said mischievously. Tau mumbled something that Giovanni couldn't hear, as he tried to rearrange his Afro to cover the spot where Giovanni had cut.

Giovanni took the chunk of hair, tied it at the cross of the divining rod, and then rushed to his potions cabinet to mix an elixir that would invoke the locater spell.

"I just got a text," Hung announced. "One of our drivers is on his way with my Mustang."

"I'm driving," Tau and Giovanni said in unison.

Chapter 11

There was an eerie calm as Zander drove up to his house. None of the family automobiles were there. His father's black Escalade was gone, and his mother's Mercedes was nowhere to be found. He parked at the beginning of the circular driveway and ran up to the house. There was no noise coming from inside—no television, no music, no singing, and no conversation.

He pulled his key from his pocket and slowly opened the door. "Ma!"

There was no answer.

"Dad!" he yelled again, and wondered where in the hell they could have gone. All of his opened birthday gifts were still piled up in the living room the same way that they had been when he left. It wasn't like his mother to leave her house so untidy. He walked through the first floor and found nothing. Every appliance and electronic item was turned off. He walked up to the second floor and found empty bedrooms. His parents' luggage was still tucked away in the closet, and none of their clothes were gone. His eyes started to water by the time he made it up to the third floor recreation room. Again, no one was there.

"Mom!" he yelled, desperately. He was beginning to feel hopeless as he headed back downstairs.

He checked the kitchen on the first floor for his mother's black cat, Tabitha, who was also surprisingly absent. Both her water bowl and food bowl were completely empty.

Zander began pacing back and forth, trying to decide what to do next. He told himself that he could figure this out. It finally dawned on him. Every magical family kept a book called a Grimoire, which contained its family traditions, spells, and potions; perhaps it would contain some secret magic way to locate his family. The Knight family's book was in the safe room, which could only be accessed through the library on the second floor. Zander took off quickly and accessed the secret doorway behind his father's collection of L.A. Banks novels. He rushed in to find that the Grimoire and their most valued family treasures were gone. The room was empty. For the second time that day, Zander fell into a heap on the floor.

Zander thought he heard a noise and looked up from his tears to find that the air was shimmering and distorted, the way it was above the asphalt on the hottest summer days. He jumped up to run out of the room and felt someone grab his shoulder. Without the proper footing, he stumbled and fell head first into the wall and knocked himself out.

Chapter 12

When Hung said he had a Mustang, Giovanni didn't know he meant a completely restored first generation 1966 Shelby GT350 with tweaked suspension and 306-horsepower 289 V8. After arguing for several minutes on the street about who was going to drive it, they had come to the conclusion that Tau needed to drive because Giovanni was the only one able to properly discern the magic in the divining rod. The gentleman that Hung had referred to as "the help" was a balding man named Thomas who looked more like a retired executive than a ghoul.

Thomas handed Tau the keys to the Mustang and nodded with indifference.

"Where might I find Master Ly?" Thomas asked, toting a Louis Vuitton suitcase in his free hand.

"Who?" Giovanni questioned.

"The dude who banged your back out last night and whose last name you don't know," Tau taunted.

"Fuck you," Giovanni answered, and turned back to Thomas. "He's in 706."

"Thank you." Thomas headed into Giovanni's building, rolling his suitcase behind him. Giovanni hadn't assumed that "the help" would be coming to his house, too, but then again he had never allowed a vampire to sleep over before. He usually required his lovers, be they shifters, warlocks, or vamps, to leave before the sun came up—literally. He couldn't help but wonder how many times Thomas had been summoned to Hung's side after a night of wild sex with a random dude.

Tau sank into the driver's seat as Giovanni invoked the power of the Y-shaped rod, which now had a sufficient amount of Tau's hair expertly knotted at its center, along with a few herbs and vines.

"I need complete quiet," Giovanni spat. Tau revved the engine and pulled out toward the highway heading south.

"I haven't told you where to go yet!"

Tau shrugged. "I know he lives in southern Georgia. It doesn't take a warlock with an old piece of wood to figure out which way to head first. You just need to let me know what to do once we get on the highway." Tau rolled down the window and turned the radio up as loud as it would go.

Chapter 13

When Zander came to, his family was standing all around. His mother, his father, his grandmother Nasha, his uncle Siran—whose wife Finity was holding a crystal globe the size of a soccer ball—and even his annoying older cousin Waverly all stood around him.

"Zandy, you really took a nasty knock to your head." His mother dabbed at his forehead with a cool, damp rag.

"We're just glad that you are all right," his Aunt Finity added. She was married to his father's brother, and Zander always admired the way she carried herself; never the one to gossip about another witch or warlock, she always came to Zander's defense when Waverly's taunting became too much to stand.

Waverly sneered. "I told you that he would run away screaming." Aunt Finity hushed him and explained that the family had covered the entire estate in protective charms, cloaking potions and illusion spells. They would be invisible to anyone outside the spell. The supernatural world was abuzz with news of the attacks, and everyone from the district coven representatives to the regional coven leader had advised congregating and going underground as quickly as possible. Technology didn't work behind the veil of such strong magic, so Zander's family couldn't send or receive calls. His parents had wanted to go looking for him, but that, too, had been discouraged under penalty of magical law.

"We prayed that you would come home," his mother cried.

"Where the hell did you go?" Waverly asked. "I looked for you all over the Litha before and after the attack."

It was easier for Zander to just not respond to Waverly. He didn't know what his parents had and had not deduced, and he didn't want to give them any more information by saying too much.

"We were worried sick about you," his father added.

Zander felt a pang of guilt. "I'm sorry. I got here as soon as I could."

"We're just glad that you're all right," Grandma Nasha replied.

Waverly sighed dramatically. "Isn't anybody curious about where he was or why he had all of us worried sick all night?"

"Now isn't the time," Grandma Nasha scolded.

"That's a nasty bump on his head, Crystal. Should I make a healing paste for him?" Aunt Finity asked, glancing periodically at her crystal globe.

His mother nodded, and Zander reached up to find a plum-sized knot on the center of his forehead, which somehow gave him a sudden headache.

"How long was I out?" Zander asked.

"Oh, not too long," his mother assured him. He could tell that she was lying. Zander looked around the room at his family. He was glad that they were safe.

"Do we know who's responsible for the attacks?" Zander tried.

His father hesitated. "Not yet, but the district coven representatives are working hard to find out."

"The regional coven representatives told us to congregate as much as possible, so we came here to be with your family," Uncle Siran added.

"So where's everybody else?" Zander asked.

His father rattled off the various places that everyone was hiding, but Zander noticed that he hadn't mentioned his Grandma Zoe. He waited a moment for his father to continue, and when he didn't, Zander finally had to say something.

"I guess Grandma Zoe was too stubborn to leave her house in Maryland, huh?" Zander tried to laugh, but it hurt. His mother burst into tears.

His Grandmother Nasha sat down on the bed and held his hand. "Zander, we can't seem to locate your Grandma Zoe."

Zander tried to sit up. "Has anyone called her house? Can't we go to Maryland?"

"The district representatives and regional coven leaders have restricted all travel," his father announced.

Grandma Nasha continued, "She was at the Litha when it was attacked."

"What was she doing there?"

"She was trying to look out for you," Waverly said.

The reality of what had happened fell on Zander like a ton of bricks. His grandmother had gone to the Litha to make sure that she could keep an eye on him. For all he knew, she might have followed them to the club to protect him and somewhere along the way gotten attacked. It was all he could do to hold the tears back in front of his family—especially Waverly.

"We've been casting a finding spell since both of you went missing. We haven't had any luck. We were only able to find your aural signature about four hours ago, and we figured then that you were headed home," his mother said, sniffling. Zander realized that his family probably hadn't been able to locate him when he was at Giovanni's house because of the charms and spells that

Giovanni had placed around the building.

"So why didn't you just meet me at the front door when I got here?" Zander asked.

"Well, we're supposed to verify everyone's identity," his father told him. "We realized it was you based on how comfortable you were in the house, but we also had to wait to make sure that no one had followed you here. And it takes a while to undo the spell that had us all cloaked in the first place."

Zander sighed. So much had changed since the last time he was home. His mother started crying again, and his aunt attempted to comfort her. The knot on his head felt like it was getting larger, and his headache was definitely getting worse. He looked at his mother, and his heart broke.

Zander leaned up to give his mother a hug. "We will find her," he whispered.

"Blessed be!" Aunt Finity shouted.

"What is it?" Uncle Siran asked, as they all looked over at her crystal globe.

"Someone is here," she whispered. "I think we are being attacked."

"You all have to lift the veil," Zander's father ordered. "Siran and I will go deal with the intruders."

"Be careful," Zander's mother pleaded.

Waverly looked at his father. "What about me? Dad, you know I can help."

"Stay here and watch over Zander," Siran ordered.

"Dammit." Waverly's shoulders dropped.

"Come, let us gather," Grandma Nasha said, speaking directly to the women. There were simply some things that witches were better at than warlocks—holding onto large spells for long periods of time was one of them. Aunt Finity gave Waverly the crystal globe and grabbed Crystal and Grandma Nasha's hands. Grandma Nasha led them into a chant, and the entire room went hazy, everything around them turning shades of black and white.

"What are you doing?" Zander asked them curiously.

Waverly rolled his eyes. "Be quiet, you idiot. They're invoking the cloaking spell"

Zander's father and uncle were both very fit warlocks and versed in most forms and aspects of magic, but neither of them had seen the soldiers that had attacked the club. When they charged out of the room, Zander wondered if they would return or meet the same fate as Milo and the security guard at Arcane.

"I can help," Zander said, trying to get up. Waverly pushed him back on the bed and scolded him for being such a nuisance.

The women were chanting and swaying. Waverly flopped down on the bed beside Zander and began looking into his mother's crystal globe. From where was sitting, Zander could also see something inside. Waverly, despite his generally bad attitude and dislike for Zander, was as adept at reading a crystal globe as his mother. Zander was again reminded of what he had missed by not going to a traditional magic school.

"What do you see?" Zander asked.

"Wait a damn minute and shut the fuck up," Waverly hissed. "They're spellcasting, and your whining is interfering."

The chanting was reaching a fevered pitch. If someone did manage to get past his father and uncle, they would have a hard time finding the rest of them unless they were very skilled magicals. Zander wished that his father and uncle had stayed with them and hidden in the room, but he couldn't really expect his father to do that. It was enough that the regional coven leader had forbidden them from going in search of his grandmother, but there was no law to say that a warlock couldn't protect his home or family.

The trio of witches finished their spell and sat on the bed, obviously exhausted.

"Dad and Uncle Mal are on different sides of the estate," Waverly said. "The two attackers won't see them coming. They're either going to whip them from both sides with wind storms or hurl boulders from the rock garden."

"Do the intruders have on uniforms?" Zander asked.

"No. I think one of them might be a... warlock. He has a divining rod," Waverly said. The room sat silent for a moment as they all crowded around the crystal globe.

Zander could barely make out the image of two men at first. And then he knew—Giovanni and Tau!

"Wait! They're my friends!" he yelled, trying to get untangled from the sheets.

"What?" his mother asked.

"It's Giovanni and Tau," he screamed.

"You can't run out there," his grandmother explained. "You're behind the veil. You can't move through it. They can't hear you or see you, either."

"Take it down, take it down. Tau is a shifter!" Zander warned. Even a warlock as powerful as his father would find it hard to defeat a shifter.

"*What?!*" his mother exclaimed. The women immediately stood, grabbed hands, and began chanting. It was powerful magic, and it couldn't be rushed.

Zander paced back and forth while the spell was being cast. He didn't dare look in the crystal globe. Instead, he looked at Waverly's reaction—and it didn't look good. His father and uncle had grown up together, so their combined magic was strong. But Giovanni was no magical slouch, and Tau was capable of turning into a wild beast that could literally tear someone's head off.

Zander's headache was getting worse, and he was starting to get dizzy, too. It seemed like it was taking a lot longer to remove the veil than it had to create it.

"A witch's work is done in a calm spirit," he heard his grandmother whisper to the others. There must have been something wrong. Perhaps they were too excited or merely too tired.

"Oh, fuck!" Waverly exclaimed.

The witches continued to chant, seeming to have gotten a second wind. The magic in the room felt strong again, and within seconds the veil and barrier were gone. They all rushed out of Zander's room and out toward the front yard.

Chapter 14

By the time they got outside, Giovanni had Zander's Uncle Siran paralyzed and suspended in midair. Zander's father had fashioned an iron bar from the estate's gate into a spear that was just inches from Tau's temple. Tau had transformed into a werelion with fully extended claws that were well within striking distance of Malachi's throat.

"Let my brother go and I won't send this spear through your friend's skull," Zander's father yelled at Giovanni.

"Fuck him and fuck you, too. I am here to save my friend," Giovanni yelled. The magical intensity in the air had his dreadlocks flying around his head like a halo. It was obvious that neither couple realized that the other was connected to Zander.

"Dad, Stop!" Zander yelled from the front door.

Zander's father turned for one split second. The momentary lapse in concentration was all that Tau needed. He snatched the spear, pushed Malachi Knight to the ground, and raised it to strike him in the heart.

"Tau, No!" Zander yelled again, before whipping his arms in an infinity pattern that sent his father, his uncle, Giovanni, and Tau flying off to separate corners of the yard. Not only had Zander broken all of their magic, but he had forced Tau to return to his human form and pinned all of them down to the ground.

"This is my father and my uncle!" Zander said, looking directly at Tau.

"How the fuck were we supposed to know that?" Giovanni asked, still attempting to get up.

"You're at my damn house. Who else would it be?" Zander yelled. The entire family was out in the front yard now, and it was a good thing that the next neighbor lived miles away.

"So is that what your family does? You attack everyone that comes to visit?" Giovanni shot back.

"Who is this?" Zander's mother asked.

"Let me up, dammit," Zander's father yelled. Zander released his hold on everyone but Tau.

"Who are these people?" Zander's mother asked again.

"They are my friends," Zander said, looking at his family, who had assembled in front of him and Giovanni.

"We can see that this... young man is a warlock, but who is the shape shifter?" his grandmother asked. If there was an issue with Zander's father's side of the family, it was that they could appear to be somewhat aloof and haughty. They were, after all, a highly respected magical family who didn't socialize with just any witch or warlock. They were very straight laced and allowed very little room for coloring outside the lines. Zander knew that to them, cavorting with a shifter was just not acceptable.

"Let me up, Zander," Tau pleaded, growing annoyed. Zander swung his arm in a wide arc, throwing Tau up in the air. Were it not for his catlike reflexes he would have fallen back to the ground. As it was, he landed squarely on his feet.

"How did you find me?" Zander asked Giovanni. Giovanni looked across the yard at his divining rod, which he had thrown down during the fight. He reached his hand out and called to it. It flew directly into his palm, and he held it up for Zander to see.

"Young man, where were you trained?" Grandma Nasha asked.

"The Erato Academy," Giovanni answered.

"Ah, Atlanta." Grandma gave Giovanni an appraising stare. The nine major private schools were named after the nine muses. There was the Erato Academy in Atlanta; the Clio Academy in Salt Lake City, Utah; the Euterpe Academy in Orlando, Florida; the Thalia Academy in New York, New York; the Melpomene Academy in Fort Lauderdale, Florida; the Terpsichore Academy in Seattle, Washington; the Polymnia Academy in Anne Arbor, Michigan; the Ourania Academy in St. Paul, Minneapolis; and the Calliope Academy in Knoxville, Tennessee.

"Will someone please explain what on Earth is going on here?" Zander's mother asked again.

"These are my friends Giovanni and Tau," Zander said, not making eye contact with either his friends or family.

"How do you know them?" she continued. Zander struggled to answer.

"You heard your mother. How do you know them?" Zander's father asked. It was apparent that he was still angry from the fight.

"I don't want to talk about it right now," Zander said, as he fought back the tears.

"You answer us right now!" his father said. The pressure was too much. Zander had experienced more drama since his eighteenth birthday than he had in his whole life, and here his father was interrogating and embarrassing him in their front yard in front of his family and friends.

"Not now, Dad," he said, lowering his voice.

"You will answer me right now, dammit!" his father yelled.

Zander exploded, "Do you really want an answer? Do you, Dad? Here you go! I met Giovanni on a gay chat site months ago. A *gay* chat site! I went to meet him after the Litha in Atlanta, and we went to a gay club. A *gay* club! This is Tau. Tau is the gay dude that I met at the gay club. A *gay* dude! I guess you could say we were dating. So there you go. I'm gay, and I am sick and tired of everyone in this damn family treating me like I'm a child. I am eighteen fucking years old, and I don't know half the spells that Giovanni does. I can barely defend myself, and I don't know shit about the supernatural community. Is that enough of a damn answer for you?"

"It was more like mating than dating," Tau corrected, as if that would help.

Giovanni rolled his eyes. "Are you serious right now?"

"I see that my little cousin has some edge to him," Waverly said, in a tone that almost sounded like admiration.

"I don't believe this. This is ridiculous. Let's all go back in the damn house right now," Zander's father ordered. His family slowly turned and went back into the house without a word, leaving Zander, Giovanni and Tau outside.

"Zander, I'm sorry, dude. We only came here to help. We were really worried about you," Giovanni said.

"I know. It's not your fault. How'd you get here, and what is that thing?" Zander pointed at the divining rod.

"Hung let us borrow his car, and this is a divining rod. We had to use magic to find you," Giovanni explained. He glanced over at Tau and then back to Zander. "I need to go... call Hung and make sure that he hasn't torn up my house." Giovanni headed back to the Mustang.

"Thank you for acknowledging me to your parents," Tau said.

"That had nothing to do with you," Zander responded hotly.

"Wait. What's wrong with your head?" Tau gently touched the knot on Zander's forehead.

"Long story," Zander responded, and then noticed the chunk missing from Tau's hair. "What's wrong with *your* head?"

"Long story. I see that you still have your ring on." Tau frowned.

"With everything that's been going on, I guess I forgot to take if off," Zander started to remove the ring.

Tau covered Zander's hand with his larger ones. "Please keep it. I want you to have it."

Zander was beginning to regret his tantrum.

"Excuse me," Giovanni said. Neither Zander nor Tau had noticed his return.

"What is it?" Zander asked Giovanni.

"You should go back in the house before your father comes back out here." Giovanni glanced warily toward the house. "He looked like he was pretty upset. Heathcliff and I can leave."

"I'm glad you came," Zander told them.

"Even me?" Tau asked, poking out his bottom lip. He was too cute for Zander to resist.

"Even you," Zander said, smiling.

Tau grinned. "I'm sorry that I wasn't more honest. I guess my heart got in front of my head."

"I'm sorry that I overreacted," Zander said. "I should have been able to use my words and not my magic to communicate my feelings."

"Tell your dad we're sorry about the misunderstanding. I'm glad to see that your family is safe. Now that you and Catwoman made up, we can get the hell out of here. I'll call you later."

"That's just it, though" Zander said. "Everything isn't okay. My Grandmother Zoe is still missing. We think she was either at the Litha or near the club when the soldiers attacked. No one can find her." Zander paused, frowning. "The ruby necklace was the last thing that she ever gave me."

"Baby, I'm sorry." Tau put his arm around Zander's shoulder, and surprisingly, Zander allowed him.

Zander's mother opened the front door. "Whatever you boys are talking about, you can talk about in the house. The entire supernatural community is suggesting that we all stay undercover." She looked at Zander and gave him a small smile. "We're about to go back behind the veil and then break bread. Your guests are welcome to stay, so come in the house."

Zander looked at Giovanni pleadingly. Giovanni sighed and nodded back, reluctantly following Zander into the house. Tau hesitated in the front yard, and Zander's mother closed the door behind her to talk to him privately.

"You do not feel comfortable here?" she asked.

"Yes, ma'am. You have a very beautiful house and a nice family... but in my kind, breaking bread with family is a part of the mating ritual, and I am not sure if Zander wants that."

"I know the ways of your kind better than you might imagine," Crystal told him.

"Again, my apologies for the fight," he offered.

"It was a misunderstanding. I am glad to see that you care enough about my son to look after him."

"Yes, I do," Tau explained.

"If you were mating with my son, then that means that you gave him something of great value to you, and he did the same," she said.

Although it wasn't a question, he responded, "Yes, ma'am."

"And did you complete the second phase of the mating ritual with my son?"

Tau hesitated, thinking of their night at Giovanni's. "Yes ma'am."

Zander's mother paused and looked back toward the house. Then she grabbed Tau's arm and walked him out onto the porch.

"My son Zander is quite unique," she explained.

"Yes ma'am," Tau said.

"I am starting to believe that his father and I made a few mistakes in raising him." She sighed. "He knows relatively little about magic, yet he is a powerful warlock. He was forced to grow up around mortals, and I see that all of this has caused him great shame and frustration."

"Are you okay with the news that your son is gay?" Tau asked.

"I suspected as much. A mother always knows. I just want him to be happy. I sense that my son is attracted to you, but there is some tension. Explain," she ordered.

"Yes ma'am. When I first saw Zander, I knew that there was something about him. He was like me but different. I can't explain it. He beckoned to me in a way that no other shifter ever has. I knew I had to meet him. I had no intentions of hurting him. I guess I got caught up. Before I knew it, I had given him my grandfather's cowrie shell, and we were making love. I thought he wanted it, too."

"My son has grown up under a shroud of secrecy and deception. He has had to hide his magical identity and his sexuality. I guess he longs for some level of truth in his life."

Tau smiled. "I think he found it today. Is his father okay with everything?"

Crystal glanced back toward the house. "Not right now. I pray that he will come around in time. He loves our son. I think he is hurt that Zander felt like he couldn't tell us. Unfortunately, secrets and lies have been a part of this family for far too long."

Tau raised his eyebrows. "What do you mean?"

"Pack law says that you must be bound in confidence when asked to do so by an elder, as long as the oath brings you no personal harm," she said.

"I mean you no disrespect, but that pack law only applies when my elder is another shaper shifter," Tau said as politely as he could.

"I know that," she said.

Tau hesitated. "What are you saying?"

"I must have your word first," she said.

"By blood and by law, my oath is given," Tau said, as was the customary way to accept the oath among shifters.

"And by law and by blood, your oath is received," she answered.

"I am not sure that I understand," Tau admitted.

Crystal looked back at the house to make sure that no one was listening. "We don't have a lot of time. I need for you to listen. This is a secret that I have kept from Zander and his father. I think it is important for you to know, especially now that my mother may be gone. If something happens to me, then I'll need you to promise to tell Zander—to help him." She took a deep breath. "My father is a shifter. He was my mother's first lover, but because of my family's station in the magical community, she could never tell anyone. Shortly after I was conceived, she married a very prominent warlock and raised me as if he were my real father. After the man who raised me died, my mother finally told me the whole truth. My mother and I have been carrying this huge secret. When I graduated from school, we lied and told everyone that I was going to Africa to train in potions work. I really went to live with my real father, who taught me the ways of our kind. So when Zander's father got fed up with the family politics and magical community and suggested that we live as mortals, I was all for it. There was less of a chance that I would ever be found out that way. I have used strong potions all of these years to keep my shifter side hidden from the magicals in my family."

Tau stared in disbelief. "Wait, wait. Do you mean to tell me that Zander is part shifter, and he doesn't know it? The first shift normally happens around 21, sometimes even sooner. Is Zander going to be able to turn? Zander's shifter grandfather is still ali—"

"Is everything alright?" Zander asked from the doorway.

"I'm just getting to know your friend," his mother replied, visibly startled by Zander's sudden appearance.

"Grandma says that it isn't safe to be outside and that you should come in the house," Zander said, looking suspiciously at both his mother and Tau. Neither acknowledged his stares. Instead, they turned and walked into the house as if they were talking about the weather. Zander's grandmother was directing everyone in the house.

"The table has been set," Grandma Nasha told them. "You can go ahead and start eating without us. We have some work to do. We will join you in moment."

Tau found a spot at the large dining room table next to Zander. Zander's father was conspicuously absent, and his uncle and cousin were staring back and forth between Giovanni and Tau. Zander's grandmother, aunt, and mother headed upstairs—presumably to replace the cover of magical protection over the house.

"So, the Erato Academy in Atlanta taught you the offensive magic that you performed in the yard?" Waverly asked Giovanni, sounding somewhat surprised.

"Yes," Giovanni answered in a very matter-of-fact tone. He had dealt with elitist assholes like Waverly at Erato, and he knew when someone was trying him.

Waverly sniffed. "I went to Thalia Academy. We didn't

really focus on offensive magic. Our curriculum was heavily weighted toward earth magic, which is, as you know, slightly more complex. I guess that's why Thalia is so highly regarded. My dad and my Uncle Siran went to Thalia, too. All of the witches and warlocks in my family went there—well, most of them." Waverly sneered at Zander.

"My father went to Thalia Academy," Giovanni told him. "He graduated first in his class. He used to brag about being a Thalia graduate until the Senior Mage got caught sleeping with a first-year witch and two of the Master Wizards got caught consorting and trading spells with demons." He reached across the table of food for a poached pair. Zander made a mental note to thank Giovanni for shutting Waverly down.

"Your father was a valedictorian at Erato?" Uncle Siran asked. "What was his name?"

"Gavin Nugent," Giovanni answered.

"Blessed be. I knew your father. He was two years behind me. I remember him to be a very fine warlock."

They slowly began to pick over the food, more out of habit and routine than hunger. Tau looked for raw meat and found none, so he made himself a salad of spinach leaves, nuts, and cheese.

Despite the fact that they were on another floor, the three witches could be heard working their magic upstairs. Their voices fell and rose with the recitation.

"Divining rod magic is more... street magic, wouldn't you say? They are teaching street magic at Erato now?" Uncle Siran asked.

"Not quite," Giovanni responded, being a little bit more respectful to the elder Siran.

"I see," Uncle Siran said.

"You look familiar," Waverly said to Tau. Tau looked up very slowly and then glanced over at Zander.

"Do I?" Tau asked.

"Where is your pack?" Waverly continued.

"Upstate New York," Tau said. Waverly gave his father a look and then glanced back at Tau.

"That is interesting because the packs in upstate New York are—"

"That's it! Why didn't I think of it sooner?" Giovanni yelled.

"What?" Zander asked, jumping in surprise.

"Not only can we find your grandmother with the divining rod, but if we reverse the magic in the ruby looking stone, then we can see her!" Giovanni yelled.

"There is a ruby looking stone?" Uncle Siran asked.

"Yes. Grandma Zoe gave it to me for my birthday," Zander said with hope bubbling up inside of him.

"Your magic will be limited behind the veil," Waverly said, almost sounding like he wanted to help.

"Then we will have to go outside the veil," Giovanni responded.

"Your father won't have it," Uncle Siran said, looking at Zander.

"My father isn't here right now, is he?" Zander snapped. Waverly nodded in admiration.

"Do you still have the stone?" Giovanni asked Zander.

"Yes. It's in my pocket," Zander said.

"What good will seeing her do? Even if you do get the reverse spell to work, you won't be able to help her," Waverly said.

"That's my grandmother. If she's alive, I am going to save her." Zander stood, with Giovannia and Tau following suit. Giovanni grabbed his divining rod from the floor.

"Let's get out of here," Zander told them.

"The veil is closing. You'll have to hurry," Waverly warned.

Uncle Siran yelled for his brother. "Malachi!"

"Let's go!" Zander yelled again.

"We won't be able to get out if the veil is closed," Giovanni said.

Waverly jumped up. "Don't worry about that. Get to the car, and I'll interrupt the spell."

"Really?" Zander asked in disbelief.

"Yes. Really, cousin." Waverly turned and ran upstairs to where the witches were still chanting.

"I cannot allow this," Uncle Siran said, just as Zander's dad, Malachi, came into the room. It looked as if he had been crying.

"What is it now?" his father asked, looking around the room.

"Zander is trying to leave to search for his grandmother," Uncle Siran reported.

"The coven leaders have forbidden travel," Zander's father scolded.

Zander glared at his father. "Well, I wasn't exactly raised as a warlock, so the coven leaders can kiss my ass."

Without a word, Giovanni bent and swung around, waving his arms in wide circles, and then magically encased Zander's father and uncle in a translucent bubble.

"What the fuck is this?" Zander's father yelled, pressing on the magical rubbery substance.

Zander smiled at Giovanni. "You really have to teach me that one day."

Zander didn't know what Waverly had done, but he heard his mother, aunt, and grandmother screeching from upstairs.

Seconds later, Waverly came running back downstairs. "You don't have long. The veil is partially closed. If you're going to leave, then you have to go now!"

"Thank you," Zander said sincerely. He paused. "Why are you doing this for me?"

"All I ever wanted was for my little cousin to have some heart. I think I misunderstood and underestimated you. It wasn't your choice to be raised this way, and you do have a little bit of swagger about you."

Siran and Malachi were trying their best to undo Giovanni's magic bubble, but to no avail.

Waverly looked at Giovanni, "More street magic?"

Giovanni smiled. "Just a little."

"You'll have to teach me that one day," Waverly said.

Just then, the witches could be heard barreling down the upstairs hallway screaming Waverly's name. "Thanks again," Zander said, glancing at his cousin.

Waverly shoved a book into Zander's arms. "Take this, and get the fuck out of here."

"What is it?" Zander asked.

Waverly rolled his eyes. "It's the Grimoire. You might need it. Mr. Magic Trick here should be able to explain some of the harder spells to you. I'll stay here and deal with the family."

Zander, Tau, and Giovanni rushed out of the house.

Chapter 15

Hung's Mustang zoomed north up the highway from southern Georgia with Tau driving, Giovanni in the passenger's seat, and Zander practically folded up in the tiny backseat.

"This is some good fucking magic," Giovanni said as he thumbed through the Grimoire. Zander sat in the backseat, still stunned at what had happened back at the house.

Tau looked at Zander in the rearview mirror. "Are you okay?"

"I don't know what I was thinking," Zander said softly.

"You were following your heart," Giovanni told him, taking a picture of one of the pages from the book with his phone.

"My parents are probably pretty mad with me right now," Zander said.

Giovanni rolled his eyes. "Please. That was mild. Let me tell you what happened to me." He took a deep breath. "I was the valedictorian for my class. The salutatorian was this bitch named Bissey, who I thought was a good friend of mine. To make a long story short, she found out that I was having an affair with our Charms & Curses instructor. She even managed to get pictures of him and me together and send them to my parents. When they found out I was gay and sleeping with one of the professors, they banished me from the house and disowned me. After that, I dropped out of school, Bissey became the valedictorian, and my professor got fired. Your situation was completely different. After you told your parents that you were gay, they went in the house and made dinner."

"And you let her get away with separating you from your family?" Tau asked.

"I thought about moving her breasts to her back and making her cootchie smell like salmon and old potato salad... but I didn't," Giovanni said.

"You can do that with magic?" Tau asked.

"No," Giovanni admitted, "but I thought about it. She really did me a huge favor. I probably wouldn't have come out or found out how my family really felt about me if not for her."

"My dad couldn't even look at me!" Zander blurted.

Giovanni smiled at him sympathetically. "He'll come around. He was just in shock. It's not every day that your son tells you he's gay and brings home a big ole shape-shifting boyfriend."

They all chuckled.

"Do you think they'll follow us?" Tau asked.

Zander sighed. "I'd like to think they cared that much, but my father's people are way too politically ambitious to break coven law, and my mother's bound by the rules set by my father. Even though her mother is missing, she can't leave the house without my father's blessing. And despite the fact that my father has chosen to raise me outside the supernatural community, he's still bound by their law."

"Here it is!" Giovanni exclaimed. "Here is the ruby looking stone spell. I think I can reverse it, but I'll need some supplies and a quiet room. I can't do it from a moving car."

"Then what do we do?" Tau asked.

Giovanni sighed. "I don't know. If Zander's grandmother is... still alive, and if she still has the looking stone, then we go get her."

"And if she isn't?" Tau continued.

"We find out who the fuck did this to the supernatural community, and we tap that ass," Giovanni said.

Zander glanced between them. "You two don't have to do this."

"We want to," they said in unison.

"Thank you," Zander said, and sat back in the cramped backseat, trying to digest it all. He had gone from being a mortal high school graduate to a supernatural bad boy in a matter of days. Although Zander suspected that Tau and Giovanni were both adrenaline junkies anxious for the next big adventure, he was glad that they were both so willing to help him. He had barely gotten to know them, and they had already proved to be more loyal than any human friend that he had from high school.

"Let's get a hotel room at the next city so Zander and I can start working on the spell and Lion King can go to the store and get us a few ingredients."

"Sure," Tau said easily. Zander suspected Tau was being so accommodating in order to get back into his good graces. Zander didn't say anything, but it was working.

"You may not be able to find one of these ingredients in the store," Giovanni warned, looking down at the Grimoire.

"Which one is that?" Tau asked warily.

"A newly rendered heart," Giovanni read from the book.

Tau grinned. "Well it's a good thing that we're out here in the country."

Chapter 16

With Zander and Giovanni tucked away at a local hotel and working on the potion, Tau left for a nearby organic grocery store to get the first few ingredients. Having noticed a horse farm a few miles back, he knew he wouldn't have a problem delivering a fresh heart.

He was about to head to the checkout counter when he noticed a bin of recently cut orchids directly next to a bin of stuffed animals. Tau dug through the entire bin before he was able to find the one palm-sized lion beanbag. He had just placed the perfect orchid in his shopping cart, when the storeowner approached him.

"Are the flowers and stuffed animal for someone special?" she asked. She was a weathered little woman with a short, gray pageboy haircut.

"Very," Tau said.

The woman nodded. "Then you should get a basket so that it'll make a really nice presentation for her. Does she like candy?"

"He," Tau corrected. The little old woman acted as if she didn't even hear him and guided him to a shelf of organic chocolates, where she recommended a gourmet bag of chocolate covered figs.

"What is her favorite color?" she asked.

"He," Tau repeated.

"How about red?" she asked.

"How about blue," Tau said, remembering that Zander had had on a cerulean blue shirt the night they met. Once he had all of the ingredients and the contents of the I-am-sorry gift basket for Zander, he proceeded to the checkout counter.

"Did you get everything you needed?" she asked, curiously surveying the contents.

"Yes ma'am," Tau said.

"I'm glad. If I didn't know any better, I would swear that someone was preparing a potion," she said. Tau just smiled and nodded. He wondered why the old witch wasn't in hiding like Zander's family, and assumed she must be out of touch with the rest of the magical community.

"It's okay. I'm a witch, and my grandson is in a different kind of relationship, too. It was frowned upon when I was a young witch, but things are different now. Love is love, and any of us is lucky to be able to find it."

"So, was it hard for him to come out?" he asked.

"Oh, he's not gay. He's seeing a shifter." She smiled and winked. It dawned on him the lengths that Zander's mother and grandmother must have gone to in order to hide Crystal's true identity. It would have taken powerful magic to conceal the fact that she was part shifter. He could only imagine how Zander would respond to the revelation. He was just coming to terms with his magical heritage.

Tau thanked the old witch for her help and exited the store. His phone rang before he could get back to the car.

When he answered it, the first thing he heard was, "Zuri Tau Long!"

"Yes, Father," he replied respectfully.

"Where the hell have you been?" his father yelled.

"Why have you not been answering my calls?" Tau's father was Zuri Omega Long, known to those in his pack as Pack Leader Long, the alpha male, or simply Omega. He was a larger, grayer, more battle-worn version of Tau. Like most pack leaders, he maintained his shifted part-human and part-animal state in order to show his control and dominance. His mane was a beautiful crown of gold and silver, and it was thought to be an honor to be chosen by him for sex and an even greater honor to be chosen for mating. As the pack leader, he could have his choice of any member of his pack for sexual pleasure, be it a male or female. Omega Long strictly preferred female feline shape shifters, although he had been known to have a few of the finer, more delicate males in his pack on occasion. He had had three mates, the first of whom was Tau's mother, Arabella, who was as beautiful and gracious as her name.

Tau had known this call was coming, he just hadn't known when.

His father rambled on. "I supported you when you wanted to go off to Africa and visit the motherland. I supported you when you said that you had no interest in females and that you would probably never give me any grandchildren. I even supported you when you said you needed to get away from the pack and take a road trip to Atlanta before the pack trials—but enough is enough! The pack leader trials and coronation are in one month, and we have a lot of work to do. You should have been back by now. You could actually become the first feline shifter to lead the largest pack in the country. Do you know what this could mean for our family? I'll ask you again—where the hell have you been?"

It was just like Tau's father to go off on a tirade and not give him a chance to explain. Tau could only imagine how his twin sister Quay was dealing with their father.

When Tau wasn't around, which was quite often, Quay was left to bear the brunt of their father's anger.

Tau sighed. "Father, I was at an underground supernatural club the other night, and it was attacked."

"I thought that was just a rumor. Are you all right?"

"I'm fine, but a friend of mine may have lost someone in the attack, and I'm helping him."

His father paused. "That is noble, but you have your own family to worry about."

"The witch and warlock community has all gone underground over this," Tau continued.

Omega snorted. "That does not surprise me. They always cower at the first sign of danger. We are shifters."

"Even the vampires are nervous about this," Tau told him.

"How do you know all of this?" Omega asked.

"You do want me to become a pack leader, don't you? Isn't it important that I forge alliances with other supernaturals?" He hadn't gotten to know Zander, Giovanni, or Hung because of any desire to become a pack leader, but his father didn't need to know that.

"So, you mean that you are still intent on competing against Benin in the pack leader trials?" Omega asked hopefully. Benin was a physically imposing canine shifter, who was believed to be the next pack leader for the region. Tau was the only thing standing in his way.

"Not only that, father, but I plan on beating him. I just need a few more days, and I'll be home," Tau said.

His father gave a hearty laugh. "Do you need me to send a few pack members to assist you?"

"Not right now, but I'll call you if I need you," Tau said. They exchanged good-byes, and Tau hung up the phone and leaned against the car.

The pack leader trials were not to be taken lightly. Normally, pack leader trials were only held if there was a challenge after the death of a reigning pack leader, but these upcoming trials were unique. Both the Northeastern United States canine and feline packs had grown, and the two groups were struggling to maintain peace.

In a daring effort to unify the shifter communities and gain unprecedented clout and control, the leader of the feline shifters, Omega, and the leader of the canine shifters, Benin's father, had agreed to combine the two packs under one leader. And since Benin and Tau had both come of age, it only made sense that they be the contenders.

A fight to the death would decide the leader, so it was no great wonder that Tau wanted to experience love and life in the time that he had left. He could be dead within the month.

Chapter 17

Zander and Giovanni had showered and eaten and were going through the Grimoire to make sure that they both understood the looking stone reversal spell. With dusk fast approaching, all they needed was the ingredients that Tau was sent to get. Zander was amazed at how much magic Giovanni knew. They sat cross-legged on one of the king-sized beds in the large hotel room that Tau had purchased, both wearing nothing but a tank top and underwear that Giovanni had packed at the last minute.

"Are you okay? I can tell that something's bothering you," Giovanni asked, still flipping through the book in amazement.

"I guess I'm just a little bit overwhelmed," Zander admitted.

"You've been through a lot. What made you come out to your family like that?"

Zander sighed. "I guess it was a combination of things. I was really mad about the fact that I'm the same age as you, but I don't know nearly as much magic as you do because of how my parents raised me. I was mad that my father tried to embarrass me in front of you and Tau. I was mad at Waverly. I was mad at the news of my grandmother. I was just fucking mad. You know what

I'm saying? I guess a small part of me figured if you could survive without your family's blessing, then so could I."

"I'm glad that I could inspire you, but this life is not easy," Giovanni said.

"Speaking of things not being easy, what do you think about me and Tau?" Zander asked.

"What do you mean?" Giovanni asked absentmindedly.

"Should I date… *mate* with him or not?" Zander asked.

Giovanni smiled. "What does your heart say?"

"I don't know what my heart says, but my ass says yes," Zander said. Giovanni, surprised at Zander's forwardness, laughed and threw the book aside.

"Tell me more," Giovanni purred. "Wasn't it your first time? Didn't it hurt?"

"It hurt like hell at first, but then I guess I got used to it. I could start to tell that it was feeling good to him, too, which only made me want to give it to him more,"

"You do know that shifters are known for polyamorous relationships," Giovanni told him.

"What do you mean?" Zander asked, eyebrows raised.

"I mean like that television show *Sister Wives* or like that episode of *Good Times* when Thelma was going to marry that African prince Ibe—that kind of thing."

Zander flopped backward on the large, fluffy pillows. "Are you sure?"

"It's what I've heard. I don't mate with shifters. I just fuck them when I can't find a vamp." Giovanni winked.

"I guess that's one more thing that I didn't know," Zander groaned.

"Speaking of shit we don't know, when is that knot on your head going to go down?" Giovanni teased. Before Zander could answer, there was a knock at the door. Both of the young warlocks readied themselves in case it wasn't Tau.

Giovanni ran to the door, his booty jiggling as he lifted up on tiptoes to look through the peephole.

"I don't see anyone," he whispered.

"Who is it?" Giovanni called aloud. There was still no response. "Do you remember the offensive spells that I taught you?" he whispered to Zander.

Zander got off the bed and positioned himself. Giovanni swung the door open, and there stood Hung, carrying his luggage and dressed all in black. Giovanni dove into his arms and wrapped his legs around Hung's waist. Hung groped and grabbed at every part of Giovanni—especially his ass.

"Did you miss me?" Hung asked, throwing his luggage into the room on the floor.

"Sure I did," Giovanni said.

"Never lie to a vampire," Hung teased, letting Giovanni drop back to the floor.

Giovanni smiled. "Okay, I was busy, but I am glad to see you now."

"How glad?" Hung asked. Zander cleared his throat.

"Hello, Zander." Hung waved.

"Hey, Hung," Zander said, jumping back up under the covers.

"Now, how glad are you to see me?" Hung asked Giovanni again.

Giovanni turned around, pulled down his shorts. "This glad."

Zander flinched when Hung bent down and clamped down on Giovanni's right butt cheek with his razor sharp teeth.

"Excuse us," Giovanni said after a moment, pulling Hung toward the bathroom.

"Don't mind me," Zander called, as he pulled the cover up to his neck and turned his attention back toward the Grimoire.

Giovanni and Hung stripped off pieces of each other's clothing with every step. It didn't take Giovanni long to get completely naked, and Hung was in nothing but boxers and a single black sock by the time they reached the bathroom.

With both of them completely naked and the bathroom door closed behind them, Hung grabbed Giovanni by his ass checks and lifted him up onto the large bathroom vanity. It was the perfect height for penetration. Giovanni's anxious hole was perfectly level with Hung's already rock hard dick. Giovanni propped his feet up onto the vanity, making his hole even more accessible to Hung.

"So you didn't think about me all day?" Hung growled.

"I was a little busy," Giovanni said between kisses. Hung licked his middle finger and slid it into Giovanni's hole. Giovanni sighed when Hung's finger entered him. Hung began working his finger around and then in and out until Giovanni started to moisten. And when he was wet enough, Hung slid in a second and third finger.

"I want you to fuck me," Giovanni pleaded.

"Do you? Do you really want me to fuck you? You didn't think about me all day," Hung teased.

"Please," Giovanni begged.

Hung eased his fingers out of Giovanni and bent down and began licking his balls and sucking his hooded dick. There was nothing quite like the rapid motion of a vampire's tongue. Giovanni grabbed Hung's head and pushed it into his crotch. Hung licked one ball, then the other, and then both. When Giovanni's balls were wet with his saliva, Hung began nibbling his way up Giovanni's shaft, sharp teeth scraping against smooth skin. The threat of Hung biting into his hardening dick was intoxicating.

Giovanni began working his hips on the vanity in

smooth, circular motions. Hung grabbed Giovanni's ass and pulled it to his face. When Giovanni least expected it, Hung bit into the large vein running on the inside of his thigh. Giovanni screamed out in pain—pain that quickly turned to pleasure as the venom from Hung's bite seeped into his blood stream.

The bite affected them both but in different ways. A warlock's blood intoxicated vampires, and a vampire's bite initially made any of its victims horny. It was a perfect combination. Before Giovanni could relax into the pleasure of Hung sucking his inner thigh and stroking his dick, Hung lifted Giovanni up off the vanity, set him on the floor, and turned him around.

Giovanni was up on his tiptoes bent over the vanity with his ass facing Hung. Hung guided his dick into Giovanni's dripping wet hole. They both melted into the sensation and moaned with pleasure.

"This is some good dick," Giovanni groaned.

"So, are you going to forget me again?" Hung's sweet, gentle rhythms turned into ass-smacking strokes. All Giovanni could think was that Hung was trying to turn him out. No, he *was* turning him out. Hung's sex and swagger were unlike any that he had ever experienced.

Giovanni's ass bounced and jiggled with each of Hung's pounds. Hung sighed each time his entire dick disappeared deep inside Giovanni's tight, wet hole. Giovanni winced as Hung smacked his ass with alternating hands on every other stroke. Their rhythm was perfect—it was slow enough for Giovanni to feel every single inch of Hung's dick, but fast enough for Hung to enjoy the friction.

It wasn't long before Giovanni felt it, that thing he loved—vampire come. It was thicker than human come, and there was a lot more of it. When Hung orgasmed, the sensation was intoxicating. Giovanni responded by ejaculating without even touching himself. Hung's full orgasm came in waves, and his body buckled each time his warm come shot up into Giovanni.

"Are you going to forget me again?" Hung asked, doubling over onto Giovanni and wrapping long arms around him.

Giovanni turned and grinned. "No, sir."

Chapter 18

Zander sat up in the bed with the covers pulled up to his neck and the Grimoire on his lap. He was listening to the lovemaking sounds coming from the bathroom. Zander had only made love once, but he knew enough to know that what was going on in the bathroom was intense and passionate. He could hear licking, smacking, slurping, slapping, moaning, and Hung continually asking Giovanni if he would ever forget him again. Zander was pretty sure that the answer to the question was a firm no.

He imagined Hung's sleek frame banging into Giovanni, and it was making him horny. Zander slid his hands into his underwear and began to gently massage his growing erection. The smell of good sex from the bathroom tickled his nose, and his own ripening scent filled the air. He threw off the cover, slipped down his underwear, and began violently stroking his dick. He was so lost in the moment, he didn't realize the banging in the bathroom had stopped until someone was banging on the hotel door.

Someone knocked on the hotel door again, and Zander stuffed his hard dick into his shorts and jumped back under the covers. The sound of running water came from the bathroom. Zander realized that Hung and

Giovanni were showering and he was the only one left to answer the door. He remembered the offensive spell that Giovanni had taught him just in case it wasn't Tau. He lifted himself up on his tiptoes and peeked through the keyhole.

"You do know that I can smell your ripe little ass through the door, don't you?" Tau grinned. Zander blushed, straightening his underwear and checking his breath before opening the door. Tau was standing there with a bag of groceries in one hand and a beautiful blue basket filled with flowers, candy, and a cute stuffed lion in the other. He handed Zander the basket.

"Is this for me?" Zander asked.

Tau smiled. "Yes, baby."

"I haven't had a chance to show you that I'm sorry for the way that I acted," Zander said, before Tau could utter a single word. Tau lifted him up with one arm and gave him a huge kiss.

"It is cool," Tau said. "I'm sorry, too."

"I should be the one giving you the gift," Zander admitted.

Tau winked. "You can give me a gift later." He smacked Zander on his round ass, sending him off toward the bed with the basket and the bag of groceries.

Just then, Giovanni came out of the bathroom wrapped at the waist with a towel. "Sylvester, I'm glad to see that you finally came back."

"Can I assume from the overall improvement in your otherwise fucked-up attitude that Hung is here and that he gave you some much needed dick?" Tau retorted.

"The only warlock that you need to be worried about getting some dick around here is wrapped up in the sheets, and from the smell of things you must not be doing your job," Giovanni spat.

"Fuck you, Glinda," Tau responded. Zander tried to

hold back his snicker.

"That is where you are wrong. Glinda was a good witch," Giovanni started.

"Gio!" Hung shouted from the bathroom.

"That's right. Run 'cause your man said run—just like a good little girl," Tau shouted.

"Later for you," Giovanni said, snatching up the luggage and running back to the bathroom.

"Why do you two fight so much?" Zander asked.

"I hate nothing worse than a mouthy bottom. That's a real turn-off for me," Tau said.

"So, what does turn you on?" Zander asked, smiling.

"I have list of things that turn me on," Tau responded.

"Do I have anything on your list?"

"You have everything on the list," Tau answered.

Zander rolled his eyes. "I'm not that special."

"You are more special than you know," Tau told him.

Giovanni and Hung came out of the bathroom dressed in brand new clothes.

"Very nice," Zander said, snuggling up under Tau on one of the king-sized beds.

"Even nicer to see that you two made up," Hung said.

"Can you get up from under Snagglepuss? We have work to do," Giovanni said.

"And I have a surprise for you," Hung said, retrieving his suitcase and revealing brand new designer outfits for each of them. "Tau, I know you've bathed, but you've had on the same clothes since the club. I thought a change might do you some good," Hung said. Dressed in black, they looked as if they could be waiters in a New York restaurant or salesmen in a high-end department store. Despite the color choice, Hung had impeccable taste. He had even remembered to get Tau pants with Lycra that would stretch when he shifted.

Zander began reviewing the spell while Giovanni laid

the ingredients out on the bed. Tau had been thoughtful enough to purchase a small cooler for the horse's heart.

"I have good news and bad news," Giovanni said.

"What's that?" Zander asked.

"I think we have everything that we need for the potion to reverse the ruby looking stone. We can even use the tub as a cauldron, and I can heat it with witch's fire," Giovanni said.

"Then what's the problem?" Zander asked.

"The potion will have to sit for eight hours," Giovanni said.

"All the more reason to get started now," Zander said.

Tau took a quick shower while the warlocks prepared and portioned each of the ingredients. Once they were done, both Hung and Tau disrobed, jumped into their respective beds, and discussed what they had learned about the attack on the club and the supernatural community's response. Zander and Giovanni took all of their supplies into the bathroom and eavesdropped on their boyfriends shamelessly.

"So, what's the human news saying about the attack on Arcane?" Tau asked Hung.

"It was a complete cover up. They reported it as an explosion in a warehouse that was being renovated into a nightclub. They even went on to say that no one was injured in the explosion because it was after work hours and empty when it happened. We both know that wasn't true." Hung sighed.

"That means that they managed to get rid of all of the bodies before the police arrived," Tau said.

"They said that it took a while for the fire department to get to the building because both access streets to the location were blocked by the time they got there," Hung said.

"I am just glad that we made it out in time. What about

any of the vehicles that were driven by supernaturals who went to the club that night?" Tau asked.

"There was no mention of them, but I've got to believe that whoever was responsible thought about that, too. Not that it matters. Most supernaturals live off the grid anyway," Hung said.

"True," Tau agreed.

Tau was snoring softly when Giovanni and Zander finally finished with the potion.

"Now we just need to wait for eight hours. Don't anyone go into the bathroom," Giovanni ordered, as they came out of the bathroom drying their hands.

"I know what we can do for eight hours," Hung said, pulling back the covers for Giovanni. Zander rolled his eyes.

"We can let me get some sleep," Giovanni pleaded. "I'm exhausted. I haven't slept since the attack on the club. I've had marathon sex, driven across the state with Hello Kitty, fought two warlocks, watched Zander come out to his family, and made the most difficult potion of my life. I am not a vampire. I need some rest."

"Then come here and lie in my arms. I'll watch over you while you sleep." Hung opened the covers once more. Giovanni smiled and took off his clothes, easing into the bed.

Zander had snuck in his own shower before they started making the potion in the bathroom. The last one up, he made sure that the door was locked and lights were turned out before easing into the bed with Tau. He wasn't in the bed two seconds before Tau rolled over and began spooning him. The pressure of Tau's large, fleshy dick against his ass felt great. As he was drifting off to sleep, he noticed that Tau's dick was getting harder and harder, but he couldn't tell if Tau was awake—or just his dick was.

He tried to ignore it, but Tau's body called to him. When Tau slowly slid down under the covers and began gently licking his hole, he knew for sure that Tau was awake. Zander tried to be as quiet as possible, but the feeling was exhilarating. Once Tau had him completely wet, he quietly returned to his former spooning position and pushed the head of his large dick against Zander's tight hole, and then in one quick motion, Tau guided his throbbing dick inside Zander. It felt like a bolt of lightning shooting up Zander's back, but he didn't yell out. Instead, he steadied himself and slowed his breathing as the monstrous dick eased inside him. He knew it must have taken a lot of effort and patience for Tau to get his entire dick in Zander, and once again Zander lay still, trying to determine the difference between the pleasure and pain. When Tau was finally nestled inside Zander, he nuzzled his mouth and nose into Zander's neck and pulled his lover close.

And that is how they slept together, with Tau's enormous dick deep inside him. Every time Zander shifted or inhaled, Tau's dick jumped inside Zander, sending impulses and vibrations through his entire body. It was the most erotic night's sleep that Zander had ever had. Witches and warlocks remembered all of their dreams in vivid detail, and Tau was in every one of Zander's dreams. The strange thing was that in every one of his dreams, it seemed like Tau was trying to tell him something, but he couldn't talk—almost as if he was bound from speaking.

Chapter 19

"Wake up! I think it worked," Giovanni yelled from the bathroom.

It was more than just a little difficult for Zander to ease Tau's large, still-hard dick out of him and then crawl out from under his massive, muscular frame. He had learned two things about sleeping with Tau last night. Tau loved to cuddle, and he was a very sound sleeper—or at least most of him was.

The daytime was when Hung normally rested, so it was no wonder that he, too, was fast asleep.

Zander found Giovanni in the bathroom, kneeling and gazing into the tub, which was completely filled with a bubbling, red liquid.

"How do you know it worked?" Zander whispered.

"The potion's still bubbling like it's supposed to. Look at the very bottom of the tub. The ruby looks like it's changing colors." Giovanni pointed.

"Why didn't you pull it out?" Zander asked.

"This is very personal magic. It's your stone and your grandmother. We want it tuned to your aural energy. You need to be the first one to come in contact with it."

Zander expected the bubbling, red potion in the tub to be extremely hot. It was, instead, ice cold to the touch. He eased his hand in, grabbed the stone, attached the leather strap, and slowly pulled it out. He peered into it. Much to his amazement, he was staring at an image of his grandmother.

"She's all right! My grandmother is alive." Zander's head swam with relief.

"Let me see," Giovanni asked, careful not to touch the stone.

"It is too bad that we can't hear her," Zander said.

"Stop being so negative and just relax. At least we can see her. The good news is that I also found a binding ribbon in the book that belonged to your grandmother. We can use it with the divining rod to take us to her," Giovanni said.

"I don't know what I would do without you," Zander marveled.

"Me either," Giovanni smiled.

"Look! She's holding up the stone and showing us where she is," Zander said.

"It looks like some kind of holding cell." The room was full of dozens of other people.

"Is that the bodyguard from the club? How did they capture her big ass?" Giovanni wondered.

"I think that is Ooba," Zander said, astonished.

"I'll get your grandmother's ribbon, fashion the divining rod, and wake up the guys if you'll clean up this bathroom," Giovanni offered.

They were all up and dressed with the room completely scrubbed of any magical residue within the hour. Zander didn't take his eye off the stone in hopes of finding some details of where his grandmother might be held captive.

"I am sorry that I can't go with you," Hung whispered into Giovanni's ear.

"I understand. You'll come to me as soon as night falls?"

"You can count on it," Hung smiled.

"And don't worry. I'll be thinking about you all day," Giovanni said, and offered his neck to Hung for a quick bite. Hung kissed his neck and sweetly declined the offer to feed from him.

"What's wrong?" Giovanni asked, rubbing his neck along his MAGIC TRICK tattoo.

"Nothing is wrong. I just want you to know that you are more than a quick high to me. We will enjoy each other later." Hung softly kissed Giovanni on his lips.

"You look worried," Tau said to Zander, who was holding the ruby in one hand and his stuffed lion in the other.

"I just hope that we can get to my grandmother in time. I've been looking at her in the stone all morning, and she's been making these weird gestures. I am afraid she may be losing her mind." Zander put his head on Tau's chest.

Tau pet his head. "I know, baby. What you are doing here is very brave. I'm proud of you." Zander leaned in to let Tau look into the stone.

Zander's grandmother, Zoe, was performing a series of unique hand gestures and movements followed by even stranger head movements.

"She doesn't normally behave that way," Zander said.

"Wait. Those are shifter signs," Tau said slowly.

"What?" Giovanni said from across the room.

"Yes, she is doing shifter signs. When we stay in our shifted state for long periods of time, we sometimes lose the ability to speak before all of our natural animal instincts kick in. The shifter signs were adopted generations ago to ensure that we could quickly communicate during the transition," Tau explained.

"So, why does Zander's grandmother know shifter signs?" Giovanni asked.

"That's not important right now. The fact that she is

131

doing shifter signs must mean that she knows that you're with me."

"Well, what is she saying?" Hung said. Tau cradled Zander's hands in his and studied the stone.

"She is referring to the Potowatomi lands," Tau told them.

"Where the hell is that?" Giovanni asked.

"In the Chicago area," Tau explained. "There are six great packs in the United States. The first is centered in Arizona, covering parts of southern California and New Mexico. The second is in Washington and Oregon. The third is here where we are in the Alabama through Florida region. There are two in the upstate New York and Maine area—one of those is mine. The sixth in centered in Chicago and includes the Great Lakes. The pack lands are designated by the Greek alphabet now, with the largest pack being the Alpha pack. They used to be called by the names of the Native American tribes. When we say the Potowatomi lands, we typically mean Chicago."

"Great. Let's head toward Chicago and then use the divining rod to hone in on the exact location when we get there." Giovanni started gathering his luggage.

"That's an eleven-hour drive from here," Tau said. "Hung, do you mind if we take the Mustang?"

"No at all. I am just bummed that I can't go with you."

Zander looked back into the stone at his grandmother who was still making the same gestures. She dropped the stone, and the view changed. Suddenly, he saw a great commotion as what looked like the same soldiers who had attacked the club rushed into the room and pulled out a young, female vampire. It was the woman who had checked their IDs at the club.

Chapter 20

The drive to Chicago was filled with conversation about everything from the supernatural community's waning numbers to the mortal population's lack of knowledge concerning the supernatural community. Tau drove the Mustang as if he owned it, Giovanni sat in the front seat reading the divining rod, and Zander sat in the cramped backseat memorizing spells from his family's Grimoire.

"Who do you think has the greater numbers? Shifters, vamps, or magicals?" Zander mused.

"It's gotta be magicals, but not by much. I bet there are no more than three-thousand supernaturals in all," Giovanni answered.

"Maybe it's a good thing that our numbers haven't grown," Tau pointed out. "The fewer of us there are, the less likely it is that we will ever be discovered."

"We haven't been discovered in all of these years, so I doubt that it will ever happen. The myths are enough to keep the humans satisfied," Giovanni said confidently.

"I hear that humans can't have sex without covering their sexual organs in plastic," Tau said.

"They're called condoms, and they keep humans from exchanging bodily fluids," Zander weighed in from the back.

"Then what's the point of sex?" Tau asked, bewildered.

"I know, right," Giovanni agreed.

"It's complicated. They can give each other diseases when they exchange bodily fluids," Zander explained.

"So how do they have children if they don't exchange bodily fluids?" Tau asked.

"They don't use the condoms when they are trying to have children," Zander answered.

"Then what about the diseases?" Tau continued.

Zander giggled. "Nevermind. Don't you ever talk to any humans?"

"Why would I?" Tau asked.

Giovanni laughed. "Humans can only have sex for a few minutes at a time, they get old and wrinkly really fast, and they are not very interesting—they have no magic. They can't even shift."

"Fuck you. Shifting is high magic," Tau said.

"Yes, but it's your only magic," Giovanni said.

"It is enough," Tau said.

"I know that's right." Zander agreed from the backseat.

"Tell him, babe," Tau said.

Zander winked at Tau's reflection in the rearview mirror before putting the book down and taking another look into the stone. "I've been trying to make this out for a while now, but I actually think I remember a few of the people from the club. Some of them have cuffs around their necks, some have bands attached to their arms, and some of them look mildly sedated."

Giovanni and Tau looked at one another.

"What does that mean?" Zander asked.

"That explains how they're holding them," Tau said.

"What do you mean?" Zander asked.

Tau took a deep breath. "The metal collars are designed to keep the shifters from turning. The collars are fit with razors inside. The minute a shifter turns and grows, the razors will cut into his jugular vein and kill him. The collar is used to contain the most despicable and untrustworthy of our species."

"A witch or warlock's blood pressure increases when he is about to do magic," Giovanni added. "The arm cuffs are probably designed to tell if anyone is about to do magic. I'm sure that they have some type of warning device or weapon attached to them, too. They probably don't suspect that your grandmother's ruby looking stone is more than just a piece of jewelry."

"There isn't much you can do to subdue a vamp," Tau continued.

"True!" Giovanni agreed.

"That's probably why they have the vamps all sedated," Tau finished.

Zander looked back into the stone. "What are we going to do when we finally find them?"

"Free them," Giovanni answered.

"Just the three of us?" Zander asked skeptically.

"Hell yes!" Giovanni and Tau responded in unison.

Chapter 21

The trio reached the Chicago suburb of Rosemont shortly after sundown.

"What is the divining rod thing saying?" Tau asked.

"Keep going north," Giovanni said.

After several more minutes and a few more wrong turns and arguments, they ended up in a parking lot on a hill overlooking an isolated medical-testing facility.

Tau peered out the window. "What is this place?"

"It's like a doctor's office. It is where humans go to find out what diseases they have," Zander explained.

"More about weak humans and their diseases," Tau said.

"There are some advantages to hanging around humans," Zander defended, as he took out his smartphone and searched for details on the building.

"This seems like a strange place to keep supernaturals," Giovanni said.

"They're here," Tau said, rolling down his window.

"How do you know?" Zander asked, still searching through the Internet for details.

"I'm a shifter. I can smell them."

"This building is owned by a Mr. Archer Carmichael," Zander read from his phone.

"That doesn't really help us much," Giovanni responded.

"It might help us if we knew why he was keeping them," Zander said.

"He's just the owner of the building. He might not even know they're being kept there," Giovanni pointed out.

"What we need to know right now is how many soldiers there are in there," Tau said.

Zander looked up from his phone. "Maybe we need to go get help."

"Incoming," Tau said. Giovanni and Zander looked at each other, confused, until Hung tapped on the passenger's window. Despite Tau's warning, it startled them both.

Giovanni threw his divining rod into the floor of the car and jumped out to give Hung a big hug.

"It looks like someone missed me," Hung said, wrapping his arms around Giovanni's waist.

"Maybe," Giovanni responded.

"Have you two forgotten what we're here for?" Tau spat.

"I'm here for this," Hung said, grabbing handfuls of Giovanni's ass.

"This is serious," Tau insisted.

"Tau is right," Hung responded, reluctantly pulling away from Giovanni. Tau and Zander got out of the car and joined them.

"We can't just go down there and knock on the door and ask if our supernatural friends can come out and play," Zander said.

"You forget who we are," Giovanni said.

"What do you mean?" Zander asked.

"My baby can survey the place for us," Giovanni said.

Hung bowed. "Your wish is my command."

"We'll sit here and wait for you," Tau said. Tau took

a seat on the ground and pulled Zander down to sit between his legs. Giovanni gave Hung a kiss on the cheek and told him to be safe. Hung was gone in a blur. Stealth was the vampires' forte; they moved at near superhuman speed and were able to bend shadow and light in ways that made their movements practically imperceptible.

Giovanni paced across the parking lot while they waited for Hung's return.

Zander turned and gazed at Tau. "I really appreciate you being here with me."

"I can think of no other place that I would rather be," Tau said.

"Really?"

"My mother says that a man may have many lovers, but that he will only have one true love," Tau said.

"And how does a man know when he has found his true love?" Zander asked.

Hung returned before Tau could answer. Giovanni showered him with hugs and kisses before he could start talking.

"Let the man breathe, Frosted Flakes," Tau said, pulling Zander up to his feet.

Hung immediately began to share everything that he had learned. "All of the activity is on the first floor. The second floor is nothing but storage. It looks like they captured eight vampires, eight witches and warlocks, and eight shifters. They are pulling them by species for some kind of tests. Of the twenty-four supernaturals that they captured, three have already been picked apart and killed, one from each species. They have removed their vital organs and are straining and examining their blood now. There is one vampiress on the examining table, and I can't tell if she's dead or alive."

"Blessed be," Giovanni and Zander said, their voices low with shock.

"So, assuming that the vampiress is alive, that means that there are twenty-one supernaturals in that building," Giovanni said.

"There are humans down there, too," Tau added. "I can smell them."

"You're right, Tau. There are twenty soldiers and six scientists," Hung explained.

As the son of a pack leader, Zander knew Tau had been trained in the ways of battle. When he showed off his training, Zander found it extremely sexy. First, he instructed Giovanni to make a witch light drawing of the layout of the building as described by Hung. The result was an illuminated floor plan that literally hung in midair. Once it was drawn, Tau made sure that each one of them knew how to find the entrances, exits, lab, and holding room. When they were done, Giovanni erased the magical drawing as easily as one might clean a chalkboard.

"We have the element of surprise on our side, but that may not be enough. Hung, disable the power in the building, and then we'll take out the soldiers and the scientists," Tau ordered.

Zander knew what Tau meant by *taking out* the soldiers and scientists, and although it was necessary, he was chilled by how casually Tau had mentioned killing. Zander had never even torn the wing off of a day fairy, let alone thought about harming another living creature. He didn't mention it. Instead, he asked, "What about me?"

"We need you to free the supernaturals. Do you have a spell that can break locks and remove the collars and cuffs?" Tau asked, as he removed all of his clothes except for the black pants that Hung had given him. Zander couldn't help but stare.

"I think I do," Zander said, regaining his composure.

"Then let's go shut this bitch down," Giovanni said fiercely. "Once we have all of the supernaturals out, we will burn this motherfucker to the ground the same way they did the club."

"I suggest we enter on the far north end of the building. I've already unlocked the door for us, and it's the closest exit to the holding cells," Hung added.

"Then let's go." Tau led the way.

Chapter 22

Zander was a nervous wreck as they made their way down the hill. The only thing that Zander had done that was even remotely close to this was playing hide and seek with his cousins, who always teamed up against him and used magic to make sure that he always lost. Upon closer inspection, the facility sat in a natural bowl, with the old, abandoned parking lot up on the hill on one side and woods on the three remaining sides.

Everyone else appeared so confident, which only made Zander feel that much more unsure of himself. Tau's suggestion to kill the power and the lights had been a good one, since all supernaturals had better night vision than humans. The black outfits supplied by Hung also helped to camouflage them as they made their way toward the unsuspecting soldiers and scientists.

Once they reached the northern entrance to the building, Hung stopped them. "Wait here while I go disable the power. I'll be right back." It didn't take long for him to return. The sound of panicked scientists and alarmed soldiers could be heard emanating from the building.

"We don't have long. Let's go," Tau said, as he transformed into the lion-like god that made Zander's heart skip a beat. Hung stepped back and moved his hands in an intricate series of motions that bent the shadows, covering him in a blanket of darkness and making him invisible. Giovanni followed with a piece of magic that created a shield similar to the protective bubble that he had created in the club.

They moved in complete silence, with Tau leading the way. The first room they reached was the holding cell, which was guarded by two of the twenty soldiers. Tau made short work of them, punching the first in the face and then using his limp body to knock the other out cold. Zander took the key off of the first soldier and immediately opened the door to the holding room.

General panic filled the room when Zander swung the door open.

"Stay calm. I am a warlock," Zander whispered, creating an arc of witch light as a safe signal.

"Zander?" his grandmother spoke up from the back.

"We're here to get you out, but we'll have to be quick and quiet," Zander told them.

"You got this?" Tau asked, giving his lover a quick pat on the ass with his large, furry paw.

"Be safe," Zander instructed Tau, before he led Hung and Giovanni up the hall.

Zander turned back to the room. "I need all of the shifters to line up first." He applied a piece of alchemical magic to their metal collars, making them brittle and as easy to shatter as glass. When he was done, he did the same thing for his grandmother's arm cuff.

"You found me," she said in tears.

"You and I have got to talk," Zander told her.

"I know," she said, as she wiped her face clean.

"What do these cuffs do?" Zander asked.

"They inject us with a deadly toxin at the first sign of a spike in our blood pressure. Most of the witches and warlocks have been meditating to stay calm," she answered. Zander knew that he had to move quickly. The mere excitement of escaping was enough to raise the average person's blood pressure, and they had come too far to lose anyone now. Zander and his grandmother started to break the cuffs with the same magic that he had used on the collars.

"I'll need all of the shifters to help carry the vamps," Zander ordered, while he led the way toward the exit door.

One especially beautiful young shifter with red hair and freckles stopped Zander. "I am glad that you and the prince came to rescue us." Zander didn't have time to figure out what that meant, but he knew he would have to ask later. The group filed out in a relatively quick fashion. Zander pulled up the rear to make sure that everyone got out safely. They were outside and up the hill near Hung's car in record time.

"I need for everyone to stay here and give my grandmother your name and contact information," Zander ordered. "I know that it isn't normal to ask for this type of information, but I may need to contact you to get information about anything that you might have seen or heard while you were captured. The more information that we have, the more likely it is that we can find out who did this." Zander gave his grandmother his phone to take names and numbers.

"Where are you going?" she asked.

"My friends are in there. I have to go help them." He gave his grandmother a quick kiss on the cheek and dashed back down the hill.

Giovanni, Tau, and Hung had already made short work of eight of the soldiers, leaving ten more somewhere in the building. Zander caught up with them right before they reached the laboratory.

"Is everyone out?" Giovanni asked.

"Yes, I have my grandmother getting their names so that we can contact them later if we need to."

"Good idea," Tau whispered. Then, he signaled for all of them to be quiet. They were stopped just outside the laboratory.

Without a word, Tau burst into the lab and scared the pure hell out of the six scientists, who were all gathered around the vampiress, Muslee. What happened next could have been a scene out of a horror movie.

The lead scientist must have assumed that Tau was one of the captives because he kept screaming, "Activate his collar!" Unfortunately for them, Tau didn't have a collar.

Tau slashed the lead scientist's throat with one stroke. Hung punched another through the chest and squished his heart before biting the third in his neck and drinking from him until the life drained completely from his body. Not to be outdone, Giovanni sent a tray full of scalpels flying through the air and into the neck of the fourth scientist. Blood spurted out like a fountain until he fell to the floor.

"Wait!" Zander said, before anyone could harm the last two scientists.

"What is it?" Giovanni asked.

"The vamps are still up on the hill and knocked out from the drugs. The blood from these last two scientists may help them recuperate faster," Zander said, amazing himself at his sudden disregard for human life. The last two scientists, one a small, balding white man and the other an even smaller Asian lady, began screaming wildly.

"Shut the fuck up," Hung said to the doctors, as he grabbed them and dragged them out toward the parking lot.

"What are you going to do with their bodies?" Giovanni asked Hung.

"I'll bring their dead bodies back inside when we're done," Hung said. To have six vampires drain two small humans promised to be a brutal and painful death. The small man screamed again, and Hung shook him until he stopped.

Zander went over to the examining table to check on Muslee. She was still alive. Zander rushed over to the computers and file cabinets and began collecting papers, reports, and jump drives.

"What the hell are you doing over there?" Giovanni asked.

"We need to figure out what they were up to. This information may help us. Giovanni, go with Hung and take Muslee and these files to the car."

"Are you sure you'll be alright?" Giovanni asked, looking over at Zander.

"Yes, just go," Zander said.

As Giovanni headed to the door, five soldiers rushed into the lab with the same rifles that Zander had seen at the club.

"Set to kill!" the first guard yelled. They all aimed at Tau, the largest and seemingly most dangerous target in the room.

Tau was fast, but not fast enough to outrun the lightning blasts emitted by the soldiers' guns. Zander had seen just one of the rifles kill Milo instantly. The blast of five was sure to kill Tau.

"No!" Zander screamed, and in a flash of magic the entire room was bathed in a white light that rearranged the soldiers like pieces on a chessboard. They found themselves all facing each other in a circle with their guns drawn, engaged and ready to fire. It was too late for them to do anything. With their guns magically trained on each other, they reluctantly watched as they fried each other to death.

"Damn!" Giovanni said, gaping and still holding the box of files that Zander had given him.

"Thanks, babe," Tau growled.

Zander smiled. "You're welcome."

Giovanni managed to get the naked Muslee up on her feet and wrapped in a sheet. Hung, however, handled the two diminutive scientists with much less care, even banging them together once or twice for good measure.

"You have no idea what you are doing!" the small woman yelled. Hung pulled her face close to his and growled at her, showing her his full fangs. She immediately wet her pants.

"We will be back soon," Hung laughed, as he and Giovanni exited.

"There should be about five more soldiers in the building," Giovanni warned as he left.

"Get the files out and bring the two scientists back," Zander instructed. "We'll burn the building down when we're done. We don't have long before the authorities come." The lab doors swung shut behind Hung and Giovanni, as the acrid smell of frying human flesh filled the room.

"Where are the last five soldiers?" Zander asked.

"It won't matter where they are if we magically seal the doors and burn the building down." Tau pulled Zander into a full and loving embrace.

"There are three doors, not counting the one that we entered. Let's go make sure they're locked and leave the way that we came," Zander said.

Zander and Tau found the first door without incident. Zander drew heat in around the metal door and its frame, permanently sealing it shut.

"Good job," Tau said appreciatively.

It felt good to use magic without limits. Zander felt free for the second time in his life. It was appropriate that

Tau was there with him, since the first time he ever felt really free was the first time he made love to Tau.

They had just sealed the second door when two soldiers confronted them.

"What are they?" the first soldier asked.

"I can't tell if it's two shifters or a shifter and a warlock," the second soldier said, pausing and giving his handheld device a puzzling stare.

The moment's pause was all that Zander and Tau needed. Tau grabbed the first guard by the neck and slammed him into the ground multiple times like an angry child would a ragdoll. Zander's approach was less violent but no less effective. He concentrated on the second soldier's helmet, reached into the air and made a fist that he closed tighter and tighter. As he did, the soldier's helmet constricted around his head until it crushed his skull like a piece of ripe fruit.

They were on their way to the third door when Giovanni and Hung found them.

"Has everyone left?" Zander asked.

"The witches and warlocks all jetted. Giving the vamps the last two scientists was a great idea." Hung smiled at Zander. "The blood gave them enough energy to get up and get away. I threw the scientists' bodies back in the lab. They both died slow and painful deaths. The shifters are another story completely. They won't leave. They said they will wait on the prince a few more minutes, and if he does not exit the building soon, they will come to help him."

"Is there something that you aren't telling us, Tau?" Giovanni asked. Zander thought Giovanni must be serious if he was using Tau's real name.

"The *prince*?" Zander asked. It wasn't the first time that he had heard the reference.

"There's no time for talking now!" Tau yelled,

exasperated. "There are still three guards somewhere in this building, and we have to get out."

Zander picked up the soldier's handheld device from the floor and stuffed it in his pocket, and the four rushed toward the exit, which was at the very end of the long corridor. They were halfway to the door when two guards stepped out from a hallway, blocking their escape. They all froze in place.

The third and final guard snuck up from the back and snatched Zander before he could respond. "If any of you move, I will fry this one's brains out!" He held the rifle directly against Zander's temple.

"Let him go," Tau roared.

"Fuck you, shifter. Revert to your human form now, or I'll kill him."

"Don't do it," Zander pleaded. The guard tightened his grip around Zander's neck.

Tau growled, slowly shifted back into his human form, and then gave the guards a mischievous smile.

"What do you want us to do?" Giovanni asked Tau in a panicked voice.

"Nothing," Tau answered calmly.

Seconds later, a group of werecreatures burst in through the northern door. Zander saw werecougars, werewolves, and even a werefox. They were all majestic and very lethal. Being a gymnast, it wasn't difficult for Zander to slip away from the distracted soldier, do two backflips, and then magically throw the guard against the wall.

"Two backflips? Really? That was such gay magic." Giovanni smiled.

The shifters took care of the rest, ripping all three guards limb from limb. When they were done with the guards, they took formation in front of Tau and bowed.

Hung whistled. "Damn!"

"Why are you bowing?" Zander asked, confused.

"Prince Tau is the son of the great Omega, leader of the Cayuga pack," the werecheetah said.

"Your father is a pack leader?" Giovanni sounded impressed.

"Within the month, our own Prince Tau will be competing to become a pack leader himself," the werecougar added.

"And he will be doing so against my own brother, Benin," said the largest of the pack. It was a huge werewolf with a streak of blond hair. It was Ooba, the guard from the club. Zander was completely confused.

"Aren't pack leader trials to the death?" Hung asked.

Zander gaped. "What?!"

Chapter 23

Zander's Grandmother Zoe was still sitting on the hill with her arm wrapped around a recovering Muslee when the group exited the building.

They all stood together on the hill as the medical facility burned to the ground. It was so isolated that no one even responded to the larger than life flames. The building and all of its contents would be long burned to ash before anyone even knew what had happened.

Of the eight shifters, two had recently moved into Tau's father's region, which meant they were now a part of his pack—the werecougar and werecheetah. Tau didn't know them, but they knew him the way humans knew and revered celebrities.

When the fire died, the remaining six shifters gave due respect and left. Ooba whispered something in Tau's ear that seemed to set him on edge. The werecougar, a twenty-five year old Puerto Rican named Kyle, and the werecheetah, a slight but buxom redhead named Chelsea, were bound to stay by Tau's side until he was safely returned to his father. It was required of any pack member to take care of royalty in that way—especially so close to the pack trials.

Muslee rose from Grandmother Zoe's embrace and returned Zander's cell phone. "I will be forever in your debt," she told him.

"Are you all right?" Zander asked her. Muslee was a short, shapely, pecan-tan vampiress with large, wide-set eyes, a cute broad nose, and full lips. Even after being held captive, she was captivating.

"I have been better," she said.

"My name is Zander," he extended his hand.

"I remember you. I am Muslee."

"Will you need help getting home?" Zander asked.

"Yes, I fear it is getting late. The sun will be up soon."

"You should all come to my house," Zander said to the crowd.

"You have a lot of drama at your crib," Giovanni teased. "Is that such a good idea?"

"We must accompany Prince Tau back to his father. It is customary that he be kept in seclusion this close to the pack trials," Kyle said.

"Let me deliver Zander to his family first," Tau told him.

"Then we will go with you," Kyle responded. Chelsea nodded in agreement.

"Muslee, are you coming with us?" Zander asked.

"If you are going to be trying to find out who did this to us and my club, then I would most certainly like to go with you," she said.

Grandma Zoe laughed. "All right then. It looks like we are going to have ourselves a supernatural party."

"There are eight of us. Even if the vamps travel back to Georgia on their own, the rest of us won't fit in a Mustang," Giovanni noted.

"There are two large buses on the other side of the building," Hung remembered.

"Perfect. I'll drive," Giovanni said.

"If you will allow it, Hung, I would like to drive back alone with Zander in your car," Tau asked.

"You can keep the Mustang for a while. I have two more just like it." Hung winked. "Look for us as soon as night falls," he told Giovanni, just before he and Muslee were gone in the blink of an eye.

Giovanni sighed. "Can we at least stop and get some alcohol?"

"Is he serious?" Kyle whispered to Chelsea.

Zander simply laughed.

Chapter 24

It was just before dawn, and the remains of the building were still smoldering miles behind them.

Giovanni drove the bus with Kyle, Chelsea, and Grandma Zoe, while Tau and Zander followed in the Mustang. Giovanni picked the nicer of the two available buses—the one outfitted with a bathroom, televisions, and plush seats. Perhaps it had been used for scientific expeditions, but it didn't matter now. The scientists wouldn't be using it.

Giovanni knew that their use of the bus would have to be temporary. Once the authorities found the burning building, they would surely complete an inventory of the facility and find the bus missing. He already knew how he would magically dispose of it once he got to Georgia, but in the meantime he would enjoy it.

There were only four of them on the large bus. Grandma Zoe was stretched out on a bed in the very back. Chelsea sat in the middle of the bus watching a movie about a lovesick mortal caught in a love triangle with a vampire and a werewolf.

Kyle sat in the first seat directly behind Giovanni, chatting with him about nothing in particular.

"How is that you and Chelsea are in Tau's pack, but he doesn't know you? There aren't that many shifters," Giovanni asked Kyle.

"Chelsea and I both recently moved into the region that Tau's father governs. Remember, that means that we're in his pack. We just happened to be at the club on the same night. Besides, Tau isn't your typical pack leader's son. He travels quite a bit. So, as new pack members move into the area, they don't always get a chance to meet him." Kyle paused. "As terrible as it was being held captive, I count it a blessing to have met Prince Tau. He is destined for great things."

"What? Why?" Giovanni looked back at Tau and Zander in the Mustang in his rearview mirror.

"Under normal circumstances, he would have just been made pack leader at his father's death, unless someone challenged him to pack trials, but this situation is a little bit different."

"How?" Giovanni asked.

"There are six great packs in the United States. Two of them are really close together up around New York. Tau's father is the leader of one of those packs. Several years ago, a deal was struck between the two packs that when the eldest sons came of age that they would compete for the pack leader position of a new combined pack," Kyle explained.

"So what does that mean?" Giovanni urged.

"It means that in a month, Tau will be competing against a werewolf shifter named Benin. If he wins, then he will be the leader of the largest pack in the country," Kyle said.

"That is some serious shit," Giovanni said.

"You ain't lying. All the power, money, and respect you could ask for. Not to mention the men that will be vying to be his first mate."

"Really?" Giovanni asked, knowing damn well that he was going to spill tea with Zander just as soon as he could.

"Most pack leaders are already mated when they assume the throne," Kyle explained. "Since Tau is still single, there will probably be several eligible bachelors seeking a seat beside him on the throne." Kyle sighed. "Enough questions about pack life. What about you?"

"What do you mean?" Giovanni asked, coyly.

"Are you serious about the vampire?" Kyle asked.

"He's just a friend," Giovanni said, not even sounding convincing to his own ears.

"That's good. Everyone knows that vampires have very short attention spans. They are only good for sex, and they get bored really easily," Kyle noted.

"Everyone knows that," Giovanni responded softly. He looked in the rearview mirror and saw Tau and Zander taking the exit. He smiled, knowing full well what they had in mind.

Chapter 25

Where are you going? The bus is leaving us!" Zander looked over at Tau curiously. They had only been driving for a few hours, and the sun was just peeking over the horizon as they neared Indianapolis on the way from Illinois to Georgia.

Tau laughed. "They're in a bus, and we're in a Mustang. I'm sure we can catch up to them after a thirty-minute break."

"Why do we need a thirty-minute break?" Zander asked innocently.

"I can show you better than I can tell you," Tau said, as he pulled off and over into a rest stop surrounded by a large wooded area. It was fairly early in the morning, so the rest stop was empty but for three or four cars. Tau pulled into a parking space, hopped out of the car and headed toward the woods without a word. Zander jumped out of the car and followed him. Tau found a clearing and started to take off his clothes. By the time Zander reached the wooded area, Tau was half naked. They were in a small clearing surrounded by a several large trees and bushes, shielded from the parking lot by foliage. The grass there was soft and cool, and it was obvious that they weren't the first two to use the space for a tryst.

Zander gaped at him. "We're in broad daylight. What the hell are you doing?"

Tau grabbed his fat, long dick at the base with his left hand and slapped it in his right palm.

"Are you serious?" Zander asked.

"Do I look serious?" Tau glanced at his dick and then at Zander. Zander eased up to him and began sucking his nipples.

"Do you remember what happened the first time we had sex?" Zander mumbled.

"Why do you think I pulled over?" Tau smiled. In one rapid movement, he threw Zander down and began ripping off his clothes. Once Zander was completely naked, Tau turned him over and began licking and gnawing at his fat, ripe ass. Tau buried his long tongue so deep inside Zander that he felt like he was getting fucked for the first time all over again. Tau's tongue was exceptionally long, and once he had it deep up inside Zander, he started to flip and swirl it around in ways that were not even humanly possible. Zander was on his hands and knees literally clawing at the earth while Tau ate him out like it was the last supper. Once Zander's ass was dripping wet with Tau's saliva, Tau stood and lifted Zander up to face him.

As they kissed passionately and furiously, Tau slowly picked Zander up and gently eased him onto the head of the massive dick. Zander locked his arms around Tau's neck, wrapped his legs around Tau's waist, and held on for dear life. Even though Tau had been inside of him twice before, Zander still wasn't completely used to the immense dick.

"Relax, baby," Tau whispered in his ear. Zander's ass was dripping wet with excitement. Tau pulled the head of his dick out and began to massage Zander's wet hole with fingers from both hands. The result was a sweet, slushy sound that made Tau want him that much more.

"You're wet for me. You must really want me," Tau whispered.

"More than you know," Zander sighed. Tau repositioned Zander again and put the tip of his dick back inside. This time, Zander buried his face in Tau's neck, pushed his hips down onto Tau's dick, grinding and gyrating. Tau responded by pumping Zander's body against his and smacking his ass.

Tau held Zander at his waist and swung his body back and forth against himself. The gentle slaps of body against body turned into loud smacks as Tau got more excited.

"You feel so fucking good," Tau moaned. Zander wriggled his hips and slid up and down Tau's cock in circular motions that tickled every nerve. Then he used the muscles in his ass to grip Tau's dick like a vice. That was a new pleasure that Tau wasn't expecting.

Rest stops were notorious for clandestine homosexual encounters, and this one was no exception. Tau noticed that two human spectators were standing there in the clearing. One was a businessman dressed in tailored suit, who obviously had not gotten what he needed at home. The other was a college fraternity guy, who looked hungover. Zander was too busy riding Tau's dick to notice anything. Tau, on the other hand, decided that if they wanted to see a show, he would give them one. Tau pulled back until his dick was almost out of Zander, then rammed in repeatedly. The smacking and sloshing was intoxicating.

The businessman and the frat boy both dropped their pants and began masturbating furiously. Tau smiled slyly before lifting Zander up and gently placing him on the ground on his back. He opened Zander's legs and guided the big dick back home. With the flexibility of a gymnast, Zander threw his ankles back up to his ears. Tau smiled and began pumping and working his way deeper and deeper inside Zander.

"Please come inside me," Zander said, still unaware that they were being watched. Tau looked up and saw the frat boy ease his way over toward the businessman and drop to his knees. After several more minutes of Tau rotating his hips and the frat boy sucking the businessman's dick, the businessman must have decided that he needed some ass, too. He threw the frat boy down and began fucking in the same position that Tau was using on Zander. They were going stroke for stroke, pounding out their respective bottoms with vengeance. The businessman was lost in the moment, having completely forgotten that he was soiling his suit. That would be the biggest mistake he made all day.

Without a word, Tau pulled his dick out of Zander, jumped up, grabbed their clothes, and snatched Zander in his arms.

By the time the police entered the clearing, Tau had shifted and climbed up into the tree with Zander. They rested several feet up in the tree between two large branches, completely hidden by leaves. Zander was still breathing hard. Tau placed his hand over Zander's mouth, making sure that he kept quiet. They watched in silence while the businessman and the frat boy got arrested for public indecency. The businessman tried to tell them what he had seen, but Tau and Zander were nowhere in sight. When the coast was clear, they came down out of the tree laughing hysterically.

"That was exciting," Zander said, trying to make sense of his shirt that had turned inside out.

"It was more than exciting. I didn't realize that you could get so wet," Tau said.

"There is one problem," Zander admitted.

"What is that?"

"Neither one of us had a chance to come before the policemen interrupted us," Zander pouted.

"So, what do you want to do?" Tau asked, grabbing his dick.

Zander threw his clothes back on the ground and turned around to offer Tau his ass. "You tell me."

Chapter 26

Word of the emancipation of the twenty-one supernaturals reached Zander's home before he did, and so did the rest of his friends. It was just a few hours before dark when Tau and Zander pulled into his driveway. Waverly was standing in the yard.

"Aren't you just full of surprises?" Waverly said, even before Tau and Zander could get out of the car.

"This motherfucker," Zander exhaled, still on edge from the taunts of his cousin. What he found, however, was a much different Waverly. This Waverly was full of admiration and respect.

"Damn, cousin! The news about what you did is all the underground is buzzing about!" Waverly said jubilantly.

"What do you mean?" Zander asked.

"You guys found out where they were holding the supernaturals, rushed the place, set them free, and then burned down the building. That is some gangsta shit right there!" Waverly said, abandoning his prep school beginnings.

Zander gaped. "How did you hear?"

"One of my friends told me that his cousin's auntie told him," Waverly said, as if that made the news more credible.

"Really?" Zander said.

"For real. And your friends are in the house. I made them tell me everything, too. The only problem is that the stories vary a little. The underground is saying that it was a few goth kids in matching uniforms who did it, but the people who were there seem to think that it was a much more organized effort."

"Maybe it's for the best that the supernatural community doesn't know the whole truth," Tau told him. "No need in alarming them for nothing. We've taken care of the problem." Zander didn't respond, but he also didn't agree. He thought that whoever had come after the supernatural community would most likely be back.

"Who's in the house?" Zander asked.

Waverly counted on his fingers. "Your Grandma Z, this fine-ass vampire chick named Muslee, your little tripped out friend Giovanni, his vampire boyfriend Hung, and two shifters named Kyle and Chelsea. Are they all gay?"

Zander rolled his eyes. "So, what did my parents say when everyone started showing up without me?"

"Well, Zander, it's been pretty rough around here," Waverly told him seriously. "After you left, your mother and father got into an argument. I don't know about what exactly, but it had something to do with a secret that your mother's been keeping from your dad. Anyway, your dad and my parents ended up leaving. I decided to stay here with Aunt Crystal until you got back. My parents were getting on my damn nerves. Then early this morning before the sun came up, the two vamps showed up. They said that the place that they'd planned to stay wasn't safe, so they came straight here. They told us they were friends of yours. I tried to call you, but you didn't answer. Your mother finally let them come in right before sunrise. We were a little bit skeptical about them until they starting telling us all about how they met you at the club."

"Great!" Zander groaned.

"Then Giovanni rolled up in a big-ass bus with two shifters and your grandmother," Waverly finished.

"Where's the bus now?" Zander asked, looking around.

"I helped Gio get rid of it," Waverly said, proudly.

"Wait. You said my parents got in a fight and my father left?" Zander asked incredulously. He had never known his parents to fight, let alone to have one of them leave.

"It was pretty serious. Your mother's been crying off and on since last night," Waverly explained.

"So, what's the underground saying?" Tau asked.

"That you're a beast... Prince Tau?" Waverly looked him up and down.

Zander glanced over at Tau. "Oh yeah, about that—"

"Zander!" his mother called from the front door. Zander turned to find his mother's eyes red and her face streaked with tears.

"What is it?" he asked meekly, sounding like a little boy half his age.

"Your grandmother and I need to talk to you."

Chapter 27

W hat the fuck do you mean I'm *part shape shifter?*" Zander's voice echoed through the large house.

"Quit cussing at me before I turn you into a salamander," his grandmother said. Zander knew that she never would.

"For all I know I might be part salamander. Neither of you would tell me," he said hotly.

"It isn't your mother's fault. You know why we had to keep the secret. But I am so sorry," Grandma Zoe said.

Grandma Zoe had always been one of his favorite people, and as far as he knew, she had never lied to him—until now.

"I hardly know how to be a warlock, and now you tell me that I am part shape shifter." Zander sighed. "So when were you going to tell me?"

"We had hoped that we might not have to. Sometimes the gift doesn't show up in those who only have a quarter shifter blood," Grandma Zoe explained.

"I guess that was another reason that I encouraged your father to move away from the magical community," Crystal admitted. "It was less likely that someone would magically sense my secret if we weren't around them so often. It has been a difficult secret to keep. I have been on a regular regimen of potions since I got married to hide it from your father."

"You always tried to act like it was my father's family who didn't want me near the magical community, but it was you two all along," Zander spat. "No wonder he left. He just found out that his son is gay and his wife is a shape shifter." Neither woman responded.

"So why now?" Zander asked.

"I knew when I saw you with Tau that he was drawn to you partly because you are part shifter. No doubt he likes you because you are attractive, but he is most likely connected to you on a species level, too. If he can sense it, then there is a pretty good chance that you are going to be able to shape shift," his mother said.

"You both are nothing but liars. All my life you have been lying to me and forcing me to lie to everyone else. I thought it was bad enough that I had to lie to all of my mortal friends, but that wasn't even the half of it. You two were lying to our entire family. The secrets have to stop now."

"We are so sorry," his mother cried.

"Are there any more family secrets that I need to know about? Who else knows this shit besides the two of you?" Zander asked. They were both silent for moments before his mother spoke.

His mother sniffed. "I told your father last night. He told his brother and Finity. I don't think they told Waverly... and Tau knows."

"What? I just met him. How does he know? Why did you tell him?" Zander asked.

"I told him to make sure that you knew in case something happened. It's pretty likely that you may be able to shift," Crystal said.

"Great! I feel like a fucking idiot," Zander said.

"Don't be mad at him. He was bound by the oath not

to tell you," his mother continued.

"What oath? You know what, don't worry about it. It doesn't matter. I don't know if I can believe anything that the two of you say anyway." Zander stomped from the room.

Chapter 28

Waverly and Giovanni were sitting directly across from each other at the dining room table, trading verbal jabs. It seemed like the only people that Giovanni didn't argue with were Zander and Hung.

Hung and Muslee were chatting and measuring the vampire community's response to the abductions, while Tau, Kyle, and Chelsea seemed to be doing the same with regard to the shifter nation. When Zander entered the dining room, everyone went silent. Without a word, Tau rushed to Zander and pulled him into a nurturing embrace. Zander had only known Tau for a very short period of time, but his arms felt like the only safe place in the world.

"Let's go outside and talk," Zander whispered, before he led Tau to his mother's garden.

Zander remembered how different his life had been the last time he was in his mother's garden. The night fairies from the garden greeted Zander with song—a song that only supernaturals could hear—and it was beautiful. It actually made him smile.

"I am proud of you," Tau said.

"What do you mean?"

"No temper tantrum this time. Your family just

dropped some pretty heavy news on you," Tau said.

"Let me start out by saying that I am really sorry about that temper tantrum that I threw at Giovanni's place. That was no way for me to act," he apologized.

Tau smiled. "Apology accepted."

"My mother told me that you were bound by some oath not to tell me that I am part shifter," Zander said.

"Yes, I was. Otherwise, I would have told you. I know how you feel about secrets."

Zander took a deep breath. "I'm afraid. I don't know who I am, what I am, or who I can trust."

"I can understand that," Tau said.

"I have a grandfather that I don't know, and my dad hates me and my mother. I can't say that I blame him. You must think that I'm a complete mess. One minute I'm making love to you, and the next I'm having a magical temper tantrum." Zander frowned at the ground.

Tau lifted his chin with a careful finger. "First, you should be excited to find out that you are part shape shifter. There are some wonderful things about shifting, and I'll teach them all to you. Second, your dad is probably just in shock. He'll come around, and if he doesn't, then so be it. Giovanni seems to be doing just fine without his parents. Finally, I don't think you are a complete mess— just a partial mess."

They both laughed, and Tau pulled Zander close.

"Those labels are for humans. Shifters are inclined to follow their instincts. We shared our bodies, but that was just a step in the journey toward sharing our souls. And if you are a mess, then so am I. I wanted it more than you did."

"I don't think that's even possible," Zander replied.

"Let's agree to disagree on that. As a matter of fact, I could use some right now," Tau said.

"We can't do that. The night fairies would be shocked

to see me getting fucked in my mother's sacred garden," Zander whispered. Tau burst out laughing again.

"What does it even mean to be part shape shifter?" Zander asked, curiously.

"Let's see if I can make this simple." Tau thought for a moment. "Back in the beginning, our blood was pure, and shifters only mated with other shifters. Over time our numbers dwindled, and shifters started mating with humans. Our blood and our gift got diluted, and some of our offspring eventually lost the ability to change."

"Why did your numbers shrink?" Zander asked.

"There were a lot of reasons. One was evolution. Some shifters started taking advantage of modern technology, no longer embracing the life of a shifter, and lost the ability to shift over generations. Then there was a brief period in our history where humans realized we existed and starting hunting us, almost to extinction."

"How do you know all this?" Zander asked.

Tau chuckled. "That's another thing. My father is a pack leader. That means that I'm sort of... kind of like... a prince. Pack royalty is obligated to train on the history of every supernatural species," Tau explained. Zander realized then that Tau probably knew more about being a warlock than he did.

"I gathered that," Zander said with a smile. "Is there a special title that I need to call you now that I know?"

"Yes, you must call me Big Daddy," Tau teased. They laughed again. The moon glowed the way that is does for lovers, illuminating everything about them.

Zander looked up at Tau. "It must be nice to be a prince. To have people adore you like Kyle and Crystal. At least you know who and what you are."

"That's just it," Tau sighed. "Being a prince means that pack law binds me. My father made an agreement a long time ago to have me compete in the pack trials when

I came of age. That time is now. I'll be competing in the pack trials in a month."

"Who will you be competing against?" Zander asked.

"A werewolf shifter named Benin. He is very highly regarded," Tau said, almost reverently.

"What happens if you just don't do it?"

"I would be expelled from the pack, and I would bring shame on my entire family. I could even be killed," Tau said, trying to soften the blow for himself and Zander.

"So, the pack trials may not be that bad. Is it like an Olympic contest?" Zander asked.

"It is a fight to the death," Tau said heavily. That was more than Zander could take. Tears were rolling down his cheeks before he knew what was happening. He had sworn to himself that he would be stronger, but he couldn't help himself.

"Baby, don't cry." Tau wiped tears from Zander's face. Zander laid his head on Tau's strong shoulder as they rocked in the swing. They sat in silence for a long while, and the night fairies' serenade become more somber.

"I don't like this," Zander said.

"Don't worry about any of the bad stuff. Just enjoy this right now. We shifters have a saying. 'Hunt for today, for tomorrow is not promised.'"

"My money is on you. You could win these pack trials, and then we can be together, right?" Zander asked.

Tau glanced away.

"Right?" Zander asked again.

"The thing about being a pack leader is that they are expected to be mated. If a newly crowned pack leader doesn't have a mate, then any shifter can compete to become his Alpha Mate," Tau explained.

"This fucking day just keeps getting better," Zander said. Then he realized why Tau was so anxious to mate with him. Tau didn't want to take the chance that someone—anyone could become his first mate. He had selected Zander. At the same time, Zander didn't know if he was ready, willing, or able to be mated to Tau for the rest of his life, given everything that he had just learned.

"So, what do we do now? What about how we feel?" Tau asked.

"I don't know. I don't have any answers right now. I want to tell you that I'll be yours forever, but my head just isn't clear right now. I need some time to get myself together," Zander told him.

"So, does that mean that we just walk away from each other?" Tau asked.

"Do we have to decide today? Do we have to decide right now?" Zander asked.

"I guess not, but we don't have long. So, what will you do now?" Tau asked, trying to change the subject.

Zander thought for several more minutes as the night fairies stopped singing. "I think I'm going to find out who kidnapped the supernaturals. It isn't like we can call the police, and I'm sure that this wasn't just a bunch of gothic kids in uniforms."

"I don't know if I want you in that kind of danger," Tau said, tightening his arm around Zander.

"Just like I don't want you to participate in the pack trials?" Zander asked.

Tau sighed. "It isn't the same."

"Isn't it?" Zander asked.

"I don't know," Tau said, and pulled his large hand through his hair.

"I may even go find my real grandfather. I bet he'll be glad to meet his gay, one-quarter shape shifting, three-quarter warlock grandson," Zander joked.

"Are you sure that the night fairies don't want to see us have sex?" Tau teased.

"Yes, I'm sure. I can't do that. They've known me

171

all my life. It would be like having sex in front of my parents." Zander shuddered.

"We kind of did that already. Remember, your grandmother had the ruby looking stone," Tau reminded him, a teasing glint in his eye. Zander swung at him, but missed. Tau was up and off the swing in the blink of an eye. Their hearty laughter filled the sky.

"About that," Zander said, as he pulled the ruby looking stone from his pocket. He tied the necklace back around Tau's neck.

"Is it mine to keep now?" Tau asked.

Zander smiled. "Yes."

"Forever?" Tau asked.

"Yes, but under one condition."

"What's that?" Tau asked.

"That you explain the shifter mating process to me," Zander said.

Tau grinned. "That's easy. First, we share personal gifts from Mother Earth. I gave you a cowrie shell from the sea, and you gave me a ruby from the earth. Second, we share our bodies. I think you remember how that went. Third, we share our families. I sat at your family table, but you have not yet met my family. Finally, we share the pledge to love eternally. It is like a ceremony. Again, the other way that a shifter prince can be mated is directly after the pack trials."

"Seems backward," Zander said, wondering if Tau wanted him to complete the mating process.

"It seems backward to you because you were raised as a human. We get the preliminaries out of the way and end with the pledge. It makes sense if you think about it," Tau explained.

Zander sighed. "I am glad that I met you."

"And I, you," Tau said. "Do you still want to wear my cowrie shell?"

Zander held up his ring finger proudly and showed off the ring.

"And I see you have on your grandmother's ruby looking stone," Tau said.

"Yes. Now you have one, and I have one. We can keep in touch supernaturally. That is, if your new mate doesn't make you take it off..."

"I wouldn't allow it," Tau said softly, and looked into the stone directly at Zander, who was also looking into his stone.

Just then all of their friends came from around the house.

"Can we crash this party?" Giovanni said. Waverly was right behind him with several bottles of alcohol that he had liberated from the family liquor cabinet. Hung played some music from his phone, and in just a few minutes, they were all laughing and dancing and singing around the garden.

Zander Knight didn't have to keep secrets any longer. He was a same-gender loving, sixth generation, part-warlock and part-shape shifter who had just graduated from a mortal high school. Zander's high school friends only knew him as the little dude with the good grades and great smile, but his new friends would come to know him for who he really was. This was only the beginning of this warlock's love story.

Epilogue

Zander and his mother moved about the house without very much interaction. She continued to make her potions, but she no longer sang the songs that he had always heard her sing growing up. He spent his days talking to Giovanni on the phone and pining over Tau. Between him and his mother, someone was always crying in the house.

Zander sat on his childhood bed with three piles in front him. To his left were all of the things that he had saved from the medical center fire before he and his friends had burned it to the ground. He had the handheld device that could identify shifters, magicals and vampires, the box of files and jump drives, and numerous Internet articles on the man who owned the medical facility, Archer Carmichael. On the right, he had a pile of maps and brochures on every major metropolitan city in the United States. And in the center sat his family's Grimoire.

His father had called back to the house several times, not to ask after him or his mother, but to demand that they give him the Grimoire. Zander had hung up the phone each time. He flopped back on the pillows and let his mind float back to thoughts of his strained family relationships, the news that he was part shape shifter, his new friends and then his beloved Tau. He thought about Tau's advice to 'hunt for today, for tomorrow is not promised,' and he knew exactly what he needed to do next.

022B/165/P